PERVERTED LITTLE FREAK

BLOOD SPLATTER BOOKS

RICK WOOD

ALSO BY RICK WOOD

The Sensitives
The Sensitives
My Exorcism Killed Me
Close to Death
Demon's Daughter
Questions for the Devil
Repent
The Resurgence
Until the End

The Rogue Exorcist
The Haunting of Evie Meyers
The Torment of Billy Tate
The Corruption of Carly Michaels

Blood Splatter Books
Psycho B*tches
Shutter House
This Book is Full of Bodies
Home Invasion
Haunted House
Woman Scorned
This Book is Full of More Bodies
He Eats Children
The Devil's Debt
Perverted Little Freak

Cia Rose
When the World Has Ended
When the End Has Begun
When the Living Have Lost
When the Dead Have Decayed

The Edward King Series
I Have the Sight
Descendant of Hell
An Exorcist Possessed
Blood of Hope
The World Ends Tonight

Anthologies
Twelve Days of Christmas Horror
Twelve Days of Christmas Horror Volume 2
Twelve Days of Christmas Horror Volume 3
Roses Are Red So Is Your Blood

Standalones
When Liberty Dies
The Death Club

Chronicles of the Infected
Zombie Attack
Zombie Defence
Zombie World

Non-Fiction
How to Write an Awesome Novel
Horror, Demons and Philosophy

CHAPTER ONE

The most remarkable thing about Briony was just how very unremarkable she was.

Most of her teachers didn't even remember her name. She wasn't smart enough to stand out, but not stupid enough to be a concern; she worked hard, but never raised her hand to answer a question; she smiled at her peers, but never grinned. Every action was discreet enough to never attract attention.

It was how she liked it.

She had grown from an introverted child to a conscientious adolescent who met every homework deadline she had ever been given. She was quietly studious, pleasantly forgettable, and even her wild ginger hair wasn't enough to get her noticed. Every parent's evening, her teachers tried to hide that they couldn't remember her name. She'd wander discreetly through the school hallways with her brown leather satchel over her dainty shoulders, her hair in two tidy pigtails, her text books clutched to her chest with anticipation of lessons to learn, her tie pulled up to her neck to ensure obedient smartness, and her knee-high socks below a knee-length plaid skirt that followed her school's strict uniform policy. She entered classrooms with her head down and her steps never loud enough to raise her teacher's eyes from their computer screen. She would softly sink into the abyss of a class filled with thirty raucous, needy students, and remain there until she was dismissed.

She had just turned eighteen. Young enough to be seen as a child, yet old enough to have a mind of her own; one that would often wander away and linger on thoughts that were just beginning to mature. She was at an age where adolescence was at its peak, and the experience of monthly menstruation was already an accustomed visit, and new feelings were surfacing about boys, and Barbies weren't cool anymore.

Not that she'd ever loved Barbies that much—which devastated her mother. Her mum had bought her an endless amount of pink outfits and cuddly toys and baby dolls ever since she was born, but Briony was far more interested in the Tonka Trucks and Action Men her twin brother played with. The only time she'd ever been noticed was at infant school, when someone had taken her brother's toy soldier away from him—she'd launched that kid across the pavement with an upper hook most boxers would be proud of. She was reprimanded by her teachers and her parents and the boy's parents —and strangers she didn't know had conversations with her about whether she ever saw Daddy hitting Mummy, and she would cry when they suggested such a thing, wailing until her Mummy and Daddy came to collect her. She quickly learned what would happen to someone who stuck out, and she learned that hard lesson at a young age.

Don't be a concern, and no one will ever be concerned.

Never get top marks, but never fail.

Never fight, and never do anything that a bully could use to victimise you.

Just remain.

Day after day, just remain.

She had a future ahead of her if she wanted it. She had a

lot of ability, despite her unwillingness to show it. She had levels of empathy that would either make her hugely caring or deviously manipulative, and she was distantly aware of it, even from a young age. She had intelligence that would make a more rebellious student seem like a troubled genius. Her life had potential without limits, with all the opportunities the possession of an inquisitive mind could bring, be it in politics or medicine or dentistry or bin removal. Whatever she wanted, she could achieve. Her parents were persistently proud of her in a way she wished they would show.

She was the girl who would write the date and title before the teacher had given the request. The girl who would keep hold of her rubbish for hours if she could not find a bin. Who would blow out her candles on her birthday cake and make a wish for someone else's happiness. Who would never ask to watch a film with an age restriction her years did not meet. Who would curl up against a cushion on the armchair and read her book whilst her brother argued about how long he was allowed to play computer games. Who would buy the cheapest clothes so she could give her change to the buskers outside the clothes shop. Whose blouse was never crumpled. Whose bed was always made. Whose vocabulary was extensive and her reading age advanced and her intentions sincere and her curiosity unbound and her desire to be loved stronger than she would ever admit.

Briony Spector was conscientiously incorruptible. Salubriously pleasant. Joyously dismal.

She was kind, shy, and unnoticed.

The kind of daughter we all wish to have.

And there was absolutely nothing wrong with her.

Nothing wrong at all.

Not even a little.

A perfectly fine, studious, smart girl.

Without even so much as a smidgen of madness.

TEXT MESSAGES RETRIEVED FROM BRIONY SPECTOR'S PHONE

I have try outs tomorrow

You didn't tell me you silly sausage!

What for?

Girls football team

You're going to rock it :) :) :)

Dunno

Amandas trying

Shes really good

And you aren't?

Dno

I think you need to believe in yourself.

You're a smarter woman than you know.

Girl

Im a girl

You're a woman, Briony.

Just because your family don't give you credit for it

How is Mum anyway?

Blurgh

Obsessed with Shane

Hes practically her full time job

That must be horrible.

I dunno

Hes always in trouble

He kinda needs it

Yes, but what about you?

Where's your attention?

That's where you come in ;)

Aw you know I'll always give you attention

My Briony

My Girl

X

XXXXXXXX

XXXXXXXXXXXXXXXX

I miss you you know.

Miss me?

But weve never met

That doesn't mean you can't miss someone.

Yeh I guess

Do you miss me?

Sometimes

I think about you a lot

What's a lot?

Like in class

At lunch

In the library

Yknow

A lot

I think about you a lot as well Briony.

I think you're the most beautiful woman I've ever seen.

Girl

You don't look like a girl to me.

I bet all the boys fancy you.

Boys dont no im here

Mum wudnt let me anyway

She gets worried wen I even speak to a boy

She is only interested when shes tellin me wot to do

Your mum doesn't know what she's missing out on.

Yeah

Wish she did though

Wish she did give me the same kinda attention she gives Shane

Not really fair

Just cuz hes trouble and Im not

You're right, it's not fair.

Not fair at all

But I'm here to make it all all right.

How are you goin to do that?

I'll kiss it better.

Kiss it?

Yes.

All over your face.

Until you laugh.

Then I'll cuddle you.

And we'll snuggle

And watch movies

Sounds perfect

That's because it is xxxx

Mum would never allow it tho

She would never let me

Like she has to know where I go

All the time

Can barely go out the door

> She doesn't need to know.

> You can say you're going to the cinema with friends.

> And we'll go somewhere else.

Where?

> Wherever you'd like.

You're funny

> Funny? : (

Yh

> You don't want it too?

Ys

Just not really practical is it

> Romeo and Juliet weren't practical!

> But they managed…

Didn't they die at the end?

> We'll change their fate.

> Have them live happily ever after!

> Keep going in secret without their families knowing.

Spose

You still haven't sent me a photo

I know my darling.

I know.

I'm insecure that's why…

You think im not?

I sent u one

I know!

And it's beautiful :)

What if you don't think I'm as good looking as you are?

I don't care

I just want to be able to picture you

Even better than picturing

Would be to see me

In the flesh

It wud.

It would.

Soon.

Soon.

CHAPTER TWO

She stood at the back of the crowd of girls. They were all so obsessed with what they looked like, tossing their blond highlights back and forth like it was a beauty pageant rather than a game of football. Even in cheap blue shorts and sickly yellow tops the school demanded they wear as their PE kit, they made an unflattering outfit look fancy with their branded sports bras and lipstick and curvy legs.

Briony looked down at her body in its shapeless form, with her bony knees, with her formless hips, with her pointy elbows, and she wondered when she would get to be a *woman*.

But she was a *woman*—Adam said she was, and he knew her better than anyone.

"Gather round!" said the PE teacher, Mrs Jones. Her tree stump legs and broad shoulders gave her an air of masculine authority. Her voice was deep and booming in a way that vibrated through your bones. No one ever dared ignore her when she demanded attention.

Once the others had gathered around Mrs Jones, Briony took her place at the back. Close enough to hear, but far enough away to avoid affecting anyone else.

"We're going to divide you into two teams, starting with you, Jemima—" She put a girl to one side of her, then a girl to the other, and she kept doing this until she reached the last girl, paused, and looked peculiarly at the small, unexceptional student before her. Mrs Jones, who had taught this student for two years, asked, "And your name?"

"Briony."

"Briony, that's it!" She snapped her fingers as if she had just remembered. She hadn't. "You join this team."

Briony looked timidly at the girls to the teacher's left and, with her head down, shuffled toward them. None of them looked at her. They were talking with an energy she could not match. They allocated each other their positions and, since they did not give Briony a place to play, she took it upon herself to play in midfield. Her favourite position.

Mrs Jones blew her whistle and, with a clipboard in hand, stood at the side of the pitch to watch the trialists perform, her judging eyes determining who was good enough to make the team. Briony was quietly confident as she had been practising for months—she'd been kicking the ball against the wall of the house and practising her first touch as it rebounded; she'd been practising keepy-uppies in the garden until she could do at least four in a row; and she'd been watching every Premier League game her brother and dad watched, but instead of shouting at the screen like they did, she'd been studying the movement of the players—where they went, how they filled the space, how they received the ball. She'd learnt how to link up with the defence to help keep possession, how to run to drag a defender out of position, and how to find the space to open up the attack.

She was ready for this.

So as soon as the game began, she was focussed, staring at the ball, tracking her teammate's movements, and making sure she did exactly as she'd seen on television.

Except she never received the ball.

She dropped deep to collect the ball in hope that she could find someone making a forward run; she made runs toward the penalty area to help the attacking phase develop; she took up a central position when the winger was about to put in a cross so she could have a shot; she dropped back when it was time to defend; stayed central at set pieces; called for the ball with a voice so quiet it was stolen by the wind—but she never received the ball. Not even once.

For the entire hour, her foot did not meet leather, and she could not show off what she'd been practising. By the time Mrs Jones blew her whistle, Briony already knew she was not in her teacher's thoughts. She had not been seen at all.

No one ever saw her.

No one ever.

No one.

Except Adam.

After an hour of getting cold for no reason, growing pimples on her legs, knees buckling, rain pelting her skin, she returned to her corner of the changing room and blocked out the loud conversations coming from the shower. She kept her body facing the wall so no one saw it, hooking her 30A bra behind her back and pulling her thick knickers up her stick-like legs.

She was shapeless. Formless. Empty. Non-existent. Not even here.

Once she had changed, she sat and stared at the wet mud draining down the tiled floor, waiting to hear the list of who'd made the team, defeated but gravely hopeful. Mrs Jones demanded silence and she received it, the other girls standing with hopeful smiles and crossed fingers. They yelped as Mrs Jones read out their names and smiled in return at her students' delight. They grabbed each other's hands and jumped up and down and squealed like piglets and congratulated each other and shared big dreams of winning matches and collecting trophies. They left with linking arms, and Briony remained sat in the corner, her body dead and empty.

She took out her phone. Opened Adam's message thread. Ran her thumb over the screen, imagining she was tracing her skin over the bumps of his face. She wished she had a photo so she could look into his reassuring eyes, but it didn't matter because she had his soul. It was there, in these messages, and she could feel it with a passion that no one could take away from her.

It was all she could hang onto.

Mrs Jones followed the girls out of the changing room and turned out the light. Briony stepped into the darkness and felt her way across the walls, grateful Mrs Jones hadn't locked the door, and left.

She put her hands in her pockets as she trudged home. Head down. Not interested in the world around her. An empty crisp packet danced along the wind, discarded and unacknowledged. A couple barged into her as they passed, too engrossed in their conversation to even realise someone had disrupted their stride.

Briony stopped and turned. Watched the couple disappear. Hands interlocked. Laughing. Joking. Infuriatingly content. Pretended it was her and Adam.

It was like all those Disney films had taught her—the answer was love. Undeniable, deep, epic, glorious love. She'd seen it in the movies. She'd seen in her parents. She'd seen it in the girls she went to school with.

But not her.

Briony was forbidden from such frivolities.

Her mother said Briony wasn't ready. That she wasn't mature enough for a boyfriend. That she wasn't old enough yet. Yet Mum never objected to all the random girls her brother brought home from school. In fact, her father often encouraged it, nudging Shane's arm and giving him a subtle wink that conveyed some sort of masculine pride. Yet Mum always told Briony she was too young. Apparently, that half an hour between the moment Shane was born and Briony was born made all the difference.

Once, Briony had even gathered the courage to ask her mum why it was different, but she'd only received that dreadful sentence that puts down and dismisses all young, inquisitive minds—*you'll understand when you're older.* Then Mum had become distracted by Shane's arrival home; she'd been waiting to reprimand him for getting suspended from school again. Their conversations were usually interrupted by whatever Shane had gotten into on that particular day. Usually, Briony let it go.

But not this time.

It was just one comment, but it was delivered with such ferocious certainty, as if it was a formidable prediction of a future cataclysmic event Mum was trying to prevent; as if Briony's fingers interlocked with a boy's fingers was a travesty that went against the laws of nature; as if the idea that a boy or man would ever wish to kiss her was sinful and abhorrent.

Briony did not want to listen anymore.

What did Mum know?

Nothing, that was what.

Adults didn't always have the answers.

Briony knew what she was ready for. She knew her own mind better than anyone. She knew what she felt.

It was her life, and Adam was the only person who treated her like she was allowed full autonomy over it. He was the one person who made her feel noticeable, or grown up, or loved.

When she came down for tea later, her mother made an announcement. "Your father and myself are going away for the weekend."

"Who's going to watch us?"

"Grandma."

Shane rolled his eyes, and Briony's instinct was to do the same. Grandma was old, smelled like cheese, spent most of the time shouting at daytime television, and often fell asleep before dinner, leaving them hungry. One time, she'd shoved twenty pounds in Briony's hand and told her to go get some candy for dinner while she smoked in the garden. When her parents arrived home, Grandma would tell them the kids had been no trouble, but they never asked the kids how Grandma had been.

She wasn't even their biological grandmother, but that was never discussed, and it became another one of those topics that Briony had learnt not to ask about.

She hated Grandma looking after them. But this weekend, she didn't mind. Because there would be an opportunity to leave without it being noticed. An opportunity to go somewhere without anyone asking questions. An opportunity to be gone for a while without it raising suspicion.

She wasn't a child anymore, and she was going to give her time to someone who realised that.

And no one needed to know.

TEXT MESSAGES RETRIEVED FROM BRIONY SPECTOR'S PHONE

I want to meet

Really?

Are you sure?

Yeh

Want to meet

This wkend

Well that's sudden!

Wonderful, I mean.

In a wonderful way.

Just fed up

Mum thinks im not allowed to date

But then my twin can

Hes a boy

Why is it different

It's not different, Briony.

Your mother is wrong.

She doesn't see what a grown up person you are.

What a wonderful young woman you have become.

Do u really mean that

Or r u like saying it

Why would I just be saying it?

Dno

I think the world of you, Briony!

I think you are magnificent!

And I would be honoured to meet you this weekend :)

Honoured?

Thats well cheesy

Yes well I mean it.

I am going to show you just what a great woman you are.

Promise?

I promise!

You deserve to know xxxx

Ok

When would you like to meet?

PERVERTED LITTLE FREAK

Dno

Like Saturday

In the shopping centre

Maybe 3

Saturday at 3 is great!

But the shopping centre is a bit crowded for me.

What about a walk in a woodland park?

Let us be nice and alone…

We can hold hands…

Get to know each other…

Even more so, I mean.

Sounds gud

But how wud I get there?

Get the bus to the bus depot.

Go out the front and I will meet you there.

I'll pick you up.

You drive?

Of course I drive.

I'm a few years older than you, remember?

Yh

I remember

Just didnt realise you cn drive

How about this then?

3 on Saturday?

Yh ok

I can't wait to see you Briony!

Cnt wait to see you too

CHAPTER THREE

S he said farewell to her parents on Friday with an enthusiasm they found odd—Briony wasn't usually so keen to have Grandma stay over—but they assumed it was simply maturity, and that Briony was taking a better attitude. She spent all evening trying to hear a movie over Grandma's snoring (she'd persuaded Grandma to watch a romcom so she could pretend the main characters were her and Adam) then put herself to bed after it finished.

She could barely sleep.

She was too excited. She'd been messaging Adam for months, and he'd said all these nice things, and made all these promises, and told her how great she was—and she believed him. Every word. And she couldn't wait to see what he looked like, how he talked, how he smiled at her, how his hand felt in hers—these were all things she'd never felt like doing before; no boy in her year had ever taken her fancy, and nor had she taken theirs. But now she pictured herself as the woman in the romcom she watched with her unconscious grandma, chased by the man who adored her.

Eventually, she fell asleep with thoughts of his chiselled chin covered in stubble, his well-dressed shirt, and the way his eyes widened when he gazed at her. She did not know if he had these features, and she wouldn't be bothered if he didn't, but she pictured them nonetheless.

The next day, her alarm clock was a welcome chime of anticipation rather than the dismal omen of school it often was. She sat up and grinned at the burst of morning that peaked through the curtains. Usually, she had to drag herself out of bed, but not today—today, the birds were singing on the tree outside her window and the sun was beaming its best rays all over the world.

She made them all breakfast. Poached eggs and bacon and sausages and fried tomatoes, served with a glass of fresh orange juice. Grandma ate it with little response, and Shane glared peculiarly at her the entire time, grunting about how annoyingly happy she was being.

When Grandma fell asleep for her early afternoon nap, Briony made her move, picking up her bag and tiptoeing to the door.

"What are you doing?"

Shane's voice halted her. She was wearing a blue dress with white spots, but she never wore dresses, and she was bouncing around with a happiness that was unlike her usual neutral demeanour—he was bound to find it strange.

"I'm going out."

"Where?"

"Town."

"With who?"

"Friends."

"You have no friends."

"Today, I do."

He grimaced. Looked her up and down, his nose curled like he was inspecting a pile of excrement.

"Why are you so happy?" he asked.

"Can't I be in a good mood?"

"You're never happy."

"I am now."

"And why are you wearing a dress?"

"Do you want something?"

He shoved his hand in his pockets, huffed, and tilted his head to the side. "I'm going to ask you this question, and I'm only going to ask you once, and whatever you say, I'll believe you."

Damn. She was caught. He knew.

Had he looked at her phone?

Would he tell Grandma? Or Dad? Or Mum?

Was he about to ruin this for her?

Her body tensed. She tried to think of a lie, and he opened his mouth, and her smile faded, and he asked…

"…Are you a lesbian?"

She shook her head and let out an almighty chuckle.

"Goodbye, Shane," she said, checking her bus money was in her pocket as she closed the door behind her.

The bus stop was a ten-minute walk from her house through the local village, and she smiled at the dog walkers and retired couples and even the teenagers as she passed them. Very few of them noticed her—even in a dress, she remained unremarkable—but nothing could destroy her spirits. Not even the grumpy bus driver who scowled at her as she handed him her change.

She'd never caught the bus before, and it was quite scary, but not in the same way that robbers or murderers or crooks are scary—it was scary in the way that trying something different was scary, that texting your crush was scary. It was a *new* scary, and she felt elated that she had done it.

She kept track of where she was through the map on her phone, checking each street name for when she needed to get off. She lifted her eyes from her screen now and then to watch people get on and off, and made guesses about who they were and where they'd come from. An elderly couple entered the bus with their feeble hands wrapped around their zimmer frames, and she imagined they had been together since they were her age. A group of rowdy teenagers wearing tracksuits and grimaces they thought made them look tough played music off their phones and snarled at anyone who frowned at them for it, and she imagined what they were like alone, that each of them was caring and lovely when they weren't part of some toxic group dynamic. A couple in their twenties walked on with a stroller, the baby fast asleep, giving them a reprieve from its crying, and she wondered if that would ever be her and Adam; would they ever have a baby together?

It was a silly thought. She knew that. But this was her first love—she had not experienced the agony of heartbreak, and she dove into it with the levels of infatuation and enthusiasm that the young do when they have no reason not to. There was no reason for her to be guarded, to hold back, and she was unable to tell herself to relax and play it cool—she only had the way he made her feel. No one had ever made her feel important before, and for that reason, he was the best thing in her life.

She identified her stop with no trouble and checked her reflection in the window as the bus drove away. She patted down her dress and straightened her hair. She didn't feel pretty—it wasn't a word anyone had ever used to describe her before—but she felt like she could be through Adam's eyes.

Then a stark, sudden thought hit—what if he didn't like her?

What if he didn't think she looked like her picture?

What if he was instantly repulsed by her?

She froze outside the bus depot, ploughing through all the dreadful possibilities, an onslaught of insecurity swarming around her thoughts.

"Briony?"

She turned around. A car had pulled up beside her, and in her panic, she hadn't even noticed.

It was a blue car. Small and cheap. The driver's window was down, and a man was looking at her.

"Gosh, Briony, it's lovely to see you. You look just wonderful."

She peered at this guy, unsure of what to say. He was older than she thought he would be. He wore a grey pin-stripe shirt tucked into his jeans, and his hair was swept to the side in a neat parting—he dressed more like her dad than her peers. His smile was genuine, and he was a little handsome, but his eyes carried the weariness of age.

"Adam?" she said weakly.

"Yes, that's me."

"I—I thought…"

"Gosh, I know I'm probably a little older than I said, but let's not let that put us off. After all, we have such a wonderful day planned. I'm looking forward to it, aren't you?"

She nodded.

She was looking forward to it.

She'd imagined walking through the park with him, hand in hand, talking about everything and nothing.

So what if he was a little older?

It didn't change the way she felt about him.

"Come on then," he said, his voice kind and friendly; he sounded like an audiobook narrator of children's books. "Get in."

Her hesitation didn't last long. She walked around the back of the car, climbed into the passenger seat, and put on her seatbelt.

TRAFFIC CAMERA IMAGE

Taken at 15:08.

Car matching make and model of car belonging to Gordon Sandwell found outside Chevy Kayliss Hotel.

CHAPTER FOUR

Adam drove in contented silence. Every so often, he would glance at Briony, give her a fatherly smile, then return his stare to the road.

She, however, kept staring at him.

He had poorly shaved stubble and bristly cheeks. At first, she'd thought he was quite toned, but the more she looked, the more she noticed a bit of a belly below the shirt—he sported what she'd heard referred to as a 'dad bod.' His movement was slow and deliberate, in a way that made him seem conscientious and kind, like he was considering everything he did to make sure he appeared well-intentioned—at least, this was how the movement seemed at first.

Noticing her staring, he reached over a hand and squeezed her leg. He asked, "So how are you?" and left his hand on the bare skin of her thigh for a few seconds before needing to change gear.

"I'm okay," she said, though her voice was small and quiet. She spoke again and ensured that she made herself audible. "So what park are we going to?"

"What's that?"

"I said, what park are we going to?"

"Sorry, I don't understand?"

"You said we were going to a park."

He took a moment to think, then said, "Oh, yes! I remember. Well, I thought it would be better if we skipped the park, don't you?"

"Why?"

"Well, I've got a lovely hotel room booked."

"A hotel?"

"Yes, you'll love it—it has an ensuite, a spa, a hot tub, a king-size bed, a big TV. You like TV, don't you?"

"I guess. I like to read more."

"Ah, yes, of course you do, I remember. Well, I think there are some books there too."

The drive continued in silence for a while longer, and she just stared at him. She had been really looking forward to the park. And now she was confused—why were they going to a hotel? Don't people usually stay overnight in a hotel? She had gotten away with leaving when Grandma fell asleep, but she wasn't sure whether she could get away with being gone overnight—Shane would notice even if Grandma didn't.

Evidently seeing that she looked a little distressed, he put his hand on her leg again and said, "What's the matter?"

"Nothing."

"What is it? Come on, tell me. I don't want my girl upset."

She enjoyed being called *my girl.* It made her feel warm. Maybe it wasn't so bad.

"I just thought we were going to the park."

"Oh, I'm sorry. I didn't realise. I just thought it would be nice for us to spend some time together alone. You know, away from other people. The park will be really busy on a Saturday as well. Don't you want to go to the hotel?"

She shrugged her shoulders.

"Tell you what, we'll go to the hotel, try it out, put on the dressing gowns and watch the TV and see what books they have—and if you don't like it, we'll go to the park. How does that sound?"

"You promise?"

He took his hand from her leg and made a cross over his chest. "Cross my heart and hope to die."

"Okay."

She felt a little better. Then she felt a lot better. Finally, she wondered what the problem had been at all.

This was Adam.

It wasn't a stupid kid at school, and it wasn't her parents, and it wasn't her teachers, and it wasn't Shane, and it wasn't her Grandma—this was Adam. The only person who had her side. Just being with him was enough.

There was just one more question she needed to ask; a question that was burning inside of her, and so she blurted it out.

"How old are you?"

"Excuse me?" he said, displaying faux shock. "How very rude!"

It made her giggle. "Really? How old?"

"Twenty-one."

She frowned. He didn't look twenty-one.

"Fine," he said. "Twenty-five."

He still didn't look twenty-five. But at least he was being a bit more honest.

"Really, does it matter?" he asks. "If you were thirty, and I was thirty-nine, would it bother you then?"

She nodded. She guessed not.

"Just relax," he said. "Let's enjoy our time together. I've been looking forward to this for so long."

She smiled. "Me too."

He smiled back.

And they sailed on together past the deep sunlight, toward

a cheap hotel behind the railway line. An advert for condoms was plastered to a billboard above it, leaving half the room shrouded in darkness, and there were barely any other cars in the car park.

ROOM BOOKING

CHEVY KAYLISS HOTEL

Sandbury Lane, Gloucester, GL60 2LT
bookings@chevykayliss.com
+44 998 645204

BOOKING DETAILS

Check in by:06-01-2023
Check out by:07-01-2023
Guests: 2 adults
Unit: Room 23

BOOKED BY

Name:Gordon Sandwell
Email address:gordonssswl@gmail.com

DESCRIPTION

1 x Night£56
0 x Breakfast£0
0 x Airport Transfer£0

Total£56

ADDITIONAL INFORMATION

Check in after 1:00 p.m.
Check out before 11:00 a.m.

CHAPTER FIVE

There was no hot tub. No books. No dressing gowns.

There was a small television with only three channels on a coffee table in the far corner. An ensuite without a shower and a toilet that gurgled every ten minutes and a bed with a disgusting floral duvet that was frayed and old in the corners.

Briony felt uncomfortable the moment Adam shut the door behind him and turned the lock.

She folded her arms around her body and ran her hands up her goose pimpled skin; it was colder in here than it was outside. He didn't seem bothered. He switched on an antique lamp in the corner of the room (antique in the sense that it was old, not expensive) and placed his bag on the floor beside the bedside table.

He turned and smiled at Briony.

"Why don't you get on the bed?" he said, his voice soft and calm. He sounded like Shane's therapist, who was always so placid and thoughtful. "Make yourself comfortable."

She didn't really want to get on the bed. The bedsheets smelt damp and the wooden frame had splinters in the corners.

She glanced over her shoulder at the door. Stared at it. Imagined just walking through it. Leaving. But she didn't even know where they were. She had no money left as she'd spent it all on the bus fare, and she wouldn't know where there was a bus stop if she did.

"Briony?" Adam said. She snapped out of a trance and turned back to him. He had taken a pair of scissors out of his bag. He held them by his side like they were a cigarette. "I said, why don't you relax on the bed?"

She edged toward the bed, her arms stiff, looking at the floor to avoid looking at him. She perched on the edge of the duvet and glared at her knees. Her legs felt so bare. She hated the dress she was wearing. She hated the shoes. She hated her hair. All of it felt tainted.

He sat on the bed beside her. Rested his hand behind her back. His other hand held the scissors.

"Why do you have scissors?"

He grinned. "It's this thing I like to do. I'll show you if you want."

"What kind of thing?"

"Lie down."

She didn't want to lie down. But he was looking at her with this... this strange, cold look. Somewhere between menace and anticipation.

She didn't want to upset him. He was stronger than her.

"Lie down, Briony."

She did as she was told and slowly lowered her back to the bed, tentatively resting her rigid body on the duvet, though her feet remained on the floor.

"All of you," he prompted. "Here, I'll help."

He lifted her feet and placed them on the bed like he was setting down a baby. Then he walked to the other side of the room and took something else out of his bag.

It was a camera.

He set it on a tripod in the corner of the room and pointed

it at her. He pressed a button and a red light came on. He watched the viewfinder for a few seconds, then returned to the bed.

"Are we just going to talk?" she asked. She wasn't sure why she was asking it or where the question had come from, it just came out.

He smiled. "You need to just relax."

He climbed over her. Sat on top of her legs. His legs on either side of her shins.

She looked at the camera, then at him.

"Why is there a camera?"

"Because I wanted to capture this moment," he said, caressing her cheek with the coarse skin of his fingers. "It's our first time. It's special. Don't you want to remember it?"

"Adam, I'm not sure I want to…"

He placed a finger over her lips and shushed her. He held the scissors aloft and opened the two blades.

"Adam?"

"Briony, you need to be quiet now."

She wanted to object. Wanted to scream out. Wanted to ask all the questions in the world—but he had told her not to and she didn't want to upset him, so she kept her mouth shut and stared at him without moving.

He placed the scissors at the bottom of her dress and cut through the fabric.

She went to ask what he was doing, then remembered she was meant to stay quiet.

He ran the scissors up the length of her dress. Over her legs. Her inner thighs. Her crotch. Her navel. Her breasts. Her neck.

He opened the split dress to reveal her body.

She was shaking. Shivering. Her whole body was a quivering mess, and he didn't seem to notice. He just marvelled at her skin, her bony formless thighs, her childish hips, her skinny belly, her small breasts in a bra that was too big.

"Briony…" he whispered. "You are beautiful."

He ran his hand up and down her body, tracing her skin with his fingers, running his fingertips around the outline of her pelvis, over her pubic hair, over her navel, over her breasts.

He cut through the middle of her bra and opened it. Her nipples were erect from the cold. He massaged them with his fingers.

"So, so beautiful."

He ran the scissors through the front of her plain black knickers and discarded them on the bedside table.

"Most beautiful girl I ever met…"

He looked over his shoulder at the camera. Then he stood and backed up out of the shot.

She went to cover her body with her arms but he shouted, "Don't!"

It was the first time his voice had risen above a dulcet tone. It was something new, something aggressive, something demanding, and in hearing it she knew for sure, if she hadn't already consciously realised it, that she was in danger.

He undid his belt. Dropped his trousers and briefs to the floor. Stepped out of them. He didn't take his top off, and it made him look weird. His penis slanted to the left like a slug surrounded by a forest of hair. He began rubbing it, and it was standing to attention like a demented soldier within seconds.

He returned to the bed and climbed over her, one hand supporting his weight and the other massaging his cock.

"Adam…" she said, but it was barely a whisper, just a silent objection she couldn't force out.

He shushed her and told her it was all going to be okay.

"Adam, please…"

He opened her legs and told her to relax.

"Adam, no…"

He entered her and it hurt; it was thick and dry like a tree stump. She groaned in pain.

"Adam, please stop…"

He whispered in her ear, "My name is not Adam."

And he moved. Up and down, up and down. Thrusting harder each time.

It felt like he was scraping her insides.

Every movement was another violation, another penetration of trauma, another unwarranted belittlement.

She dropped her head to the side and sobbed.

He didn't seem to care. In fact, he didn't even look at her. He buried his head in the pillow beside her, and he was grunting, and shoving harder and harder, and getting further and further in.

She shut her eyes. Tight. Tighter. But it wasn't doing anything. So she opened her eyes again, turned her head to the other side, and stared at the red lettering of the numbers on the alarm clock, at the faded lampshade over a single bulb, at the flakes of dust on the wooden drawers—and that was when she noticed the scissors.

The sharp blade.

The pointed end.

He fucked her harder. And harder. And harder.

And she stopped crying.

And she grew angry.

Angrier than she had ever realised she could be.

It was something new. Something unspoken. Something she couldn't articulate.

It was carnal. Something untamed. Feral.

It rose inside of her, travelling up her belly, her spine, her gullet, expanding, full of fire, effervescent, a distorted contortion of something primal and savage, something hidden, something she had never felt before.

It took control of her. Demanded of her. Possessed her. Like claws gripping her arms, fixing their nails into her muscles, shooting flames across the prison of her flesh.

It glowered. It roared. It rumbled.

A beautiful monster exploded from within.

She stretched her arm toward the coffee table.

Scrambled her fingers over the handle of the scissors.

Wrapped her fist around them.

And she swung the blade as hard as she could into his neck.

999 CALL TRANSCRIPT

Automated Message
999 emergency, which service do you require?

Receptionist
Police.

Call Handler
Hello, can I take your address?

Receptionist
Yes it's Chevy Kayliss Hotel (…) it's the one on Sandbury Lane.

Call Handler
Okay (…) and what is the issue?

Receptionist
Yeah (…) I just heard all these screams coming from a room (…) just screams and screams and (…) screams.

Call Handler
Okay (…) how long have these screams been going on for?

Receptionist

I don't know (…) I wasn't sure I heard them right (…) I (…) I guess seconds (…) no (…) maybe a minute.

Call Handler

And are these screams still going on now?

Receptionist

[Pause] Yeah.

Call Handler

How many people do you think are screaming?

Receptionist

I don't know (…) maybe one (…) no more than two.

Call Handler

Do you think these are men's or women's screams?

Receptionist

Woman first (…) then (…) it's a man (…) more recently it was a man but (…) but er (…) not sure at first.

Call Handler

And what's your name?

Receptionist

It's [redacted] (…) I wasn't even meant to be in today but [redacted] called in sick (…) I think I can hear them again.

Call Handler

Okay [redacted] (…) a unit is on their way now (…) which room is it?

Receptionist
Room 23 (…) it's on the ground floor.

Call Handler
That's great [redacted] (…) they have their lights on so should be there in a few minutes.

Receptionist
Okay (…) thank you.

Call Handler
Until then I'd recommend staying where you are (…) are you safe?

Receptionist
Yes (…) I (…) I'm in the reception area.

Call Handler
Can you lock the door?

Receptionist
Yes.

Call Handler
I'd recommend doing that [redacted] (…) the police will be there soon and they will check the area.

Receptionist
Okay (…) thank you.

CHAPTER SIX

Stab slice slash fucking scum stab slice slash
there was no sense to it
no coherent thought
no rationale
no decisions
no awareness
no deliberation
she swung the scissors at his neck again
and again
and again
and again
until his body flopped over her and she was squashed
beneath it suffocating beneath it and she pushed it and it was
heavy but she pushed it harder and managed to roll out from
beneath it until she could climb over his back and plunge the
blade down into his
back his
spine his
back his
spine his
flesh his

back and

into his skin and this time she held it there and twisted it and pushed it in and dug it in and held it there and twisted it and

she could not remember when he'd stopped screaming

but she was screaming

like a banshee

like a wild beast

like a psychotic murderer possessed by violence

and the blood was over her

all over her

dripping down her face dripping down her body dripping down her chest dripping down her navel dripping down her hips dripping down her vulva

her thighs were least covered

she plunged the blade into the back of his waist and a spurt of blood sprayed over her thighs like a jet of thick mud and now all of her was covered

and it dripped

down her face

down her body

down her chest

down her navel

down her hips

down her cunt

down her thighs

and the walls the floral wallpaper the disgusting sickly pattern were a mixture of revolting beige and glorious red

and she stabbed and she held it and she dragged it down until his skin opened and his muscles opened and blood dribbled out and she could see the inside of his muscle and it looked like strings just like in biology class

she was hacking away at a cadaver and it was a hugely educational experience just stabbing and slicing and stabbing and slicing and she laughed

she actually laughed

the screams that had started

were now laughter

then they were screams again

and silence was denied and chaos reigned

she was the queen of the kingdom and the kingdom was bloody

and she stood and she turned him over and his dead eyes had rolled upwards and they were pointing in different directions and this made her even more disgusted and

she stuck the blade into an already open wound

hacking

until she could see his ribs

concealing his heart

just a glimpse

just a little bit

the red spongy exterior of his aortic pump

and she stuck the scissors in them

and she left them there

and she stood

panting

heart punching

body sweating

blood dripping

down her face

down her body

down her chest

down her navel

down her hips

down her flower

down her thighs

down her toes getting caught between the cracks thick like

ice cream dripping slowly its thickness heavy until she was a painting of epic slaughter

And then the door burst open.

Police charged in.

One of them put their arms around Briony and pulled her away and took her outside. A blanket was waiting for her. They placed it around her shoulders and told her it would be okay now, everything would be fine, they were here, it was over.

And she sat on the edge of the backseat of the ambulance, her bare feet still outside, resting uncomfortably against the bumps of the tarmac.

As she sat there, watching the rush of officers, one of which was talking to her though she didn't register what they were saying, she was brought back to this world. Her mind left its abandoned state and she returned to her body where the consequences awaited her.

She looked at her hands. Opened her palms and marvelled at the brutality.

She turned to the police officer who stood next to her. The one who was talking. They suddenly fell silent.

"What happened?" Briony asked, though her voice was quiet and distant.

"You were attacked," the officer said. "You fought him off. You did really well. It's okay now."

"You mean, I'm not in trouble?"

The officer smiled, which Briony thought was strange. "Would you like some water?" she asked.

This didn't answer Briony's question, but she was so parched she didn't care.

"Yes please," she said.

The officer stepped away and returned with a bottle of water. She watched the commotion as the police coerced a crowd of voyeurs away and put police tape around the room.

"Come on," said the officer. "Let's go to the hospital—you don't need to see this."

She helped Briony move her feet inside the ambulance and the paramedics shut the door. Briony took a large gulp of the water as she was driven away. She looked down at her hands and stared at the blood. It had dried and crusted. It was like at primary school when PVA glue got stuck to her fingers. She used to love picking it off.

She tried picking the blood off her fingers and found it even more satisfying.

SCENES OF CRIME REPORT

Supervising Inspector: DCI Kevin McCluskey
Report Completed by: Samuel Laurence

INCIDENT REPORT

Case No.
1657489-454-2023

Report Date:
06-01-2023

Report Time:
16:42
Arrival Time:
16:50
Reporting Channel:
The 999 Police Emergency Line

Location of Incident:
Chevy Kayliss Hotel, Sandbury Lane,
Gloucester, GL60 2LT

RICK WOOD

Reporting Officer:
P1678254
D324552

Reporting Witness:
[Redacted]
Reporting Witness ID:
JIFD:
H935455(M)
Victim/Reporting Witness Relationship:
Hotel receptionist

REPORTING OFFICERS' NARRATIVE:

Responded to 999 call from the receptionist
at Chevy Kayliss Hotel at 16:42 with
reports of screaming. He could not identify
the sex of the screams. Arrived at 16:50 to
Room 23 on the ground floor. A dress, bra
and woman's underwear were on the floor.
The front of each was cut open. A man was
on the bed, unclothed, with multiple lacer-
ations on his chest and neck, and scissors
lodged in his chest. He was pronounced dead
at the scene. A teenage girl, unclothed,
had blood on her face, torso, legs, arms,
and in her hair. She was taken to the
hospital by an officer. A video camera was
in the corner of the room and captured the
entire incident.

Case Classification:
Dead Body Found
Sexual Assault

Responsible Unit:
Crime Gloucestershire Region

CHAPTER SEVEN

B riony laid in the hospital bed, being doted upon by nurses and officers and doctors, fetching her food, checking she was okay, giving her water, making her cups of tea. She even had a private room with her own television, a view of the city outside, a bed she could lift up and down with a remote, and a seat where her mother could sit.

Her mother was called straight away, and she arrived with her hands clasped over her mouth. She doted upon Briony with routine hugs, and Briony wasn't too bothered, as she was busy watching a daytime television show where a couple were arguing about which of them had cheated. Her mum sat on the chair beside her, and Briony mostly ignored her, just as she was so often ignored.

But then something happened that was quite special.

Something Briony wasn't expecting.

Her mum reached her hand over, placed it on Briony's lap, and grabbed Briony's hand in hers—with an emphasis on *grabbed*. She wasn't just holding it; she was clinging on for dear life, wiping her eyes with the sleeve of her other arm.

Briony couldn't help thinking… *Oh my God, does she care?*

Briony couldn't remember the last time her mother held

her hand. She must have been an infant—and even then, it would have been to stop her from running across the road. That she was so upset astounded her—Shane was the one her mother cried over, not her. Yet here they were, Mum sat beside her, clinging onto her, clutching her daughter's hand as if they would fall away from each other if she didn't.

Briony wanted to say something, but she wasn't sure what. Maybe something reassuring. She opened her mouth but didn't form words. She soon lost her chance as the door opened and an officer strode into the room.

"Briony," the woman said, smiling like Briony's maths teacher did when someone answered a question incorrectly. "How are you?"

Briony shrugged. "I'm okay."

"I'd be surprised if you were okay," the officer said. "You've been through quite an ordeal."

The officer left a silence and Briony wondered if she was supposed to fill it. Then the officer continued talking, and Briony assumed she wasn't.

"My name is PC Tracey Cliff, but you can call me Tracey— I'm here to guide you through what happens next."

Tracey looked at Briony in the way one might look at a widow at a funeral, then took her into another room where she was told they had to prepare the rape kit. She found this strange, but she didn't question it, and did as she was asked. They took her underwear from her, put it in a bag, then made her lie back on a bed that wasn't very wide and open her legs. A nurse put some things inside of her and it was uncomfortable, and Briony didn't like it.

But her mum held her hand for the entire time.

The entire time.

As horrible as it was, she could go numb to it; she was too busy gazing at her mother, who kept reassuring her that everything will be okay in the softest voice, over and over, everything will be okay, everything will be okay. She even brushed a few strands of loose hair from Briony's sweaty fore-head, and she wondered if this was what life would be like if Shane didn't steal her mum's attention all the time.

She had never felt neglected or rejected, but she had never felt loved either. Not like this. And now the focus was on her, and she felt light and free, and she didn't want it to end.

She stayed in the hospital for another week, and it all went by in a blissful daze. A woman who said she was a child psychologist came to see her a few times, though Briony didn't like her as she smelt like garlic, and she answered her questions with as few words as possible in the hope that she'd leave.

Mum rarely left—at night, she slept on the chair beside her daughter, and during the day, she popped out to find what-ever magazine or food Briony had asked for. Mum even brought a Blu-ray player from home to connect to the televi-sion, along with Blu-rays of her favourite movies.

Briony was sad on the day they told her she was ready to go home—although she wouldn't be going home straight away, as she had to go by the police station first. Briony found this odd, as police officers had already spoken to her several times, once to take her statements and a few more times to ask questions, always accompanied by that Tracey woman.

But Briony didn't mind, as she thought it would be exciting—but the inside of the police station wasn't what Briony expected it to be. TV shows had made her think there'd be loads of detectives gathered around a pin board trying to solve a case, or dishevelled officers sweating from the heat of aggressive interrogations. In reality, it was mundane—a few officers sat at desks, clicking their mouse or typing on their keyboard, and a few wandered in whilst sipping coffees. Briony and her mother only saw this for a few seconds, as they were guided to a separate room where they were asked to sit and wait.

The room had a grey carpet, and a wall that was half white

and half blue. There was a voice recorder on a desk and two plain chairs on either side. There was a window, but the blinds were down, and the grey wall of the adjacent building blocked any light that might enter. It wasn't an exciting room, or a calming room, or a messy room—it was just a room. Recently decorated, but in drab shades of emotionless colours. There was little about it to make her excited to be in a police station as she and her mum sat down and waited for an officer to join them. Eventually, Tracey appeared, and Briony wondered why this woman didn't have anything better to do.

"Hello, Briony," she said. "You're looking well."

Briony shrugged.

"I'm going to introduce you to DCI Kevin McCluskey." Briony noticed an older male officer behind her. "He is taking over this case. And he must be good, as your mother requested him specifically."

Briony glanced at her mother, who gave her a knowing look.

"Good evening, Briony," DCI Kevin McCluskey said as he sat opposite her. "I haven't seen you since you were about this high." He held his hand out at the height of the chair, then smiled solemnly at her mother. "My parents used to be friends with your grandparents a long time ago." He turned his solemn smile to Briony. "You can call me Kevin. Can we get you anything? Water? Tea? Coffee?"

Briony shook her head and studied the police officer she was to call Kevin. He was a large man with broad shoulders and a moustache. He looked older than her dad, but fitter. He sat with his legs wide apart and one hand on his knee, leaning toward her with an intense stare that was somewhere between reassuring and discomforting. He looked like an older version of the boys at school who played rugby.

"We understand you've been through a lot," Kevin said. "And this is a difficult experience for you. And I know that you've already given statements and answered lots of questions. But, if it's okay with you, we could do with getting more of your account while it is still fresh in your memory. This might mean repeating a lot of what you've already said, but I just need to hear your account myself. Would you be okay with that?"

Briony looked at her mum, who looked back with weak eyes, then turned to Kevin and nodded.

"Of course, we will talk to you more over the coming weeks as memories fall into place, but for now, why don't you start by telling us how you knew Gordon?"

"Gordon?" she said. "Who's Gordon?"

"The man who was in the room with you."

"He said his name was Adam."

Kevin and Tracey exchanged a look.

"He told you a lot of things that weren't true," Kevin said. "Why don't you tell us what happened with the man you knew as Adam?"

She told them.

Everything.

How they met online. How they spoke. The kind of things he said. The way it made her feel. The way he understood her. The plans to meet. The plans to go to the park that didn't happen. The meeting in the hotel room. The camera. The thrusting. The scissors.

And the way it ended.

Her mother tried to hide her reaction but did an awful job. Briony could feel her mum flinching through the hand that held hers so tightly. She could hear the small breaths she tried to stifle. She could see the shudder of her shoulders and the way she covered her eyes until she stopped sobbing.

"I see," Kevin said after it was all finished. "This is a really horrible thing to have happened to you, Briony. I hope you know that."

Briony shrugged. "I liked him originally. I thought he was nice."

"Briony, do you know why he had the camera with him?"

Briony shook her head.

"You're not the only girl he's done this to. In fact, we have found videos of other girls in other hotel rooms just like yours."

Her mum covered her face. Briony just kept watching Kevin.

"We also want to reassure you that there will be no charges brought against you," Kevin said. "In fact, we admire your bravery for standing up for yourself, and I think your mother will be really proud of you."

Briony glanced at her mum. Proud? Her mum? She had never spoken such words. Yet her mum nodded, stifling tears as she gave a few jilted but definite movements of her head to confirm that yes, she was proud.

"Very," she added through the sobs.

Briony felt warm inside, a happy glow, a boost of happiness she hadn't felt before.

"Mostly, I need you to understand that this wasn't your fault." He left a silence, like she was meant to confirm that she knew this. She didn't.

The moment they stepped out of the police station, her mum wrapped her arms around her and gave her a big hug. Her mum's arms were warm and strong. She kissed her daughter's head, then she hugged her even tighter.

It was like nothing Briony had ever felt before.

EXTRACT FROM BLOG 'GLOUCESTERSHIRE AND THE GLOBE.'

TEEN TITAN FIGHTS OFF PERVERTED PREDATOR

Police were called to Chevy Kayliss Hotel in South Gloucestershire after the receptionist reported hearing screams. When they arrived at approximately 4.30 p.m. yesterday, they could not have anticipated what they were to find.

The 18-year-old girl who remains unidentified (yes I know she's been identified on social media, but some of us obey the law you know!) was found to have fought off her rapist in an act that many are hailing as 'heroic'.

The man, who was announced dead at the scene, had introduced himself to his victims as 'Adam', though the police have identified him as 43-year-old Gordon Sandwell from Bristol. Under his online disguise, Sandwell groomed many vulnerable teenage girls and lured them to hotel rooms, where he filmed their rape and posted it on the dark web for a large paying audience. Sandwell had set up a camera in the corner of the room to film his victim's rape, just as he had on several occasions before, which captured the entire exchange—from the girl's molestation to her gallant defiance in the face of a predator.

Police revealed they found videos of similar attacks on his personal devices that they could link to five other cases. They confirmed that they have notified those five victims.
After luring her to the hotel room and assaulting her on the bed, the girl used the same pair of scissors the man had used to cut open her clothes to stab him. She fought with determination and resilience until her attacker could no longer hurt her.

Police have been quick to announce that there would be no prosecution against the unnamed girl, as it would not be in the public interest to bring further trauma to a teenage girl who was evidently acting in self-defence.

Follow our live feed for further updates..

CHAPTER EIGHT

DCI Kevin McCluskey's drive home that morning felt flatter than usual.

Not that the drive home following a night shift was ever a particular joy—he would pass parents dragging their kids to school and dead-eyed office workers in smart clothes starting their commute as he was arriving home for bed. Even so, he would usually have music on, such as a compilation disc called *Happy Songs* Janine had bought him on their anniversary.

But not today.

This day, the face of a young eighteen-year-old girl remained in his mind. A girl who had not only survived a violent attack, but had responded with similar levels of violence that would leave trauma that would never heal. She would be an adult, still affected by this, and no matter how many crimes he helped to prevent, it was nights like this that clouded how he saw his job.

Every shift consisted of one painful debacle after another.

He pulled into the driveway. Took his briefcase and stepped out of the car. Waved at his neighbour who was getting into his Porsche, then unlocked the front door and entered his quiet home.

Janine wasn't up yet. He didn't blame her. There was once a time when she would wait up all night, keen to see how he was, hiding her tiredness with a smile. She'd stopped doing this years ago, but it wasn't because their love was any less. In fact, if anything, their love had grown more with age, and as they'd entered their fifties together, their affection for one another had grown deeper and more meaningful.

She didn't wait up anymore because she hated witnessing what this job did to him. It hurt her too much.

And he didn't blame her.

The mornings he would come home with stories of fisticuffs with pimps, or children taken from homes where they were being abused, or another man who'd murdered his wife, or a knife that had been pulled on him, or another injury he'd taken from some arsehole who wanted to sneak up on him and throw a punch to avenge a vendetta against the institution he worked for… they became too much.

They weren't every morning, but they were enough to create a cynic out of him, and just as he didn't come home with enthusiasm to tell his stories anymore, she didn't wait with enthusiasm to hear them. His higher rank in the force meant he had more responsibility now. People could die because of his decisions. And he didn't want her to share the burden that was placed on him.

Today, he felt like doing something kind for her. So he made her breakfast. He put bacon on the grill, sausages in the oven, and mushrooms in the frying pan. Then, as he waited for the food to cook, his absent mind drew his gaze to the kitchen drawer. He opened it. It contained diaries from decades ago, and receipts from businesses that didn't exist anymore, and old birthday cards beneath that, and boxes of expired paracetamol, and then, right at the bottom… the picture of the scan.

He checked over his shoulder to see if she was coming. She wasn't. Not that she didn't know about this too. He saw her gaze lingering on this drawer when she thought he wasn't looking. Her eyes would glaze over, a little moisture in the corner, then she'd put on her disguise and ask him a question to distract her mind.

The picture itself wasn't that great. All baby scans look the same. And this was an old one, a few decades old now, and though the picture was faded and the memory had grown vague, he still often wondered what his daughter might have been like if she'd have lived past her first day.

Brave. Strong. Powerful.

A feminist who wouldn't take shit from any guy.

A smart academic who was naturally gifted in science.

A sporty young woman who ran marathons for charity.

Whoever she'd have been, she'd have been his. But all he had were memories he'd made up to fill the blank spaces where real memories should be. His only actual memory of her would always be of the loose, stillborn body in his arms before she was taken away.

He waited to hold her again, but he never did.

Footsteps on the stairs made him hurry to put the picture back, shut the drawer, grab the spatula, and be turning the mushrooms as she entered.

"Good morning," his wife said, walking in with her fuzzy dressing gown on and her hair in clumps. He took her in his arms and kissed her.

He always loved her most in the morning.

"How was your shift?" she asked as she opened the coffee machine and poured in some beans.

"Rough. A teenage girl was attacked in a hotel room by a bloke who'd groomed her online."

"Oh gosh, is she all right?"

"She is. He isn't."

"What do you mean?"

"She killed him. Self-defence."

He took a plate from the cupboard and scraped the mushrooms onto it, then removed the bacon from the grill.

"Are you kidding?" she said. "How is she doing?"

"She seems fine now, but who knows how she will be in time."

"What a horrid experience."

"Thing is, she… she was strong, this one. A fighter. She'd have been about her age, and I wondered…" His voice trailed off. It took a lot of courage for him to broach this subject with her. "Whether our daughter would have been strong like her."

Janine bowed her head. "Oh, Kevin…"

Feeling the urge to change the subject, he handed her the plate and said, "Sausages are in the oven, just need a few more minutes."

"You not having anything?"

"I'm not hungry. Think I'm just going to bed."

"Are you sure?"

He kissed her, and it felt just as wonderful as it did the first time he'd kissed her, back when they were too young to know what life was like. There was something innocent about it. It reminded him of a time before life had beaten and battered him,

"Yeah, I'm sure."

He hurried upstairs, shut the bedroom door, closed the blackout curtains, removed his suit, and climbed into bed.

He let himself cry. Not for too long, just a few minutes. Just enough to purge a little sadness.

Then he put on his eye mask and tried to convince himself he would be able to sleep.

COMMENTS BELOW NEWS ARTICLE WITH TRENDING HASHTAG #BELIKEBRIONY

A new feminist icon #hero #ThatsMyGirl #BeLikeBriony

First Viriginia Wolf, Simone de Beauvoir, Michelle Obama…. Then BRIONY #oneofus #inspiration #BeLikeBriony

We should all raise our daughters to KICK ARSE like BRIONY #BeLikeBriony #FeministRevolt

This has changed things—now male predators will be made to fear US #NotAloneAnymore #BeLikeBriony

I wish I'd had the guts to rip my groomer apart #hero #gutsgutsguts #NeverAgain #BeLikeBriony

All men are pigs—hail briony #BeLikeBriony #GirlPower

My lecturer called me darling today n I told him to fuck himself—thank u Briony 4 giving me the strength #BeLikeBriony #ThisGirl-HasAVoice

Went out clubbing tonight and walked all the way home in a short dress, alone, at 3 am—I wouldn't have done it if it weren't for you #ThankYou #ThankYouBriony #Inspired #NotAfraidAnymore #BeLikeBriony

Fk da patriarchy #BeLikeBriony

N she's just 18… im 45, a survivor, n too scared to be alone with a man. My dad wont have a hold on me anymore—im going on a date tomorrow n im not afraid #BeLikeBriony #Survivor #NotAfraidAnymore

Wish I'd gutted my abuser. He wasn't even charged and his wife still dont know. He has three daughters. But no more #ThankYou-Briony #TomorrowsAnotherDay #BeLikeBriony

Being a woman has new meaning today. If a 18 yr old girl isn't afraid then neither am I #Briony #BeLikeBriony #BrionyYour-ABabe #BrionyIsMyGirl

A 18 yr old did what we all wanted to do… fair play to you #BeLikeBriony

We need to make this girl an icon like NOW #BeLikeBriony #Icon #Inspiration

What an amazing act of courage—to overpower her rapist like that. Wow. Just… wow #amazing #briony #belikebriony
Can you get an OBE at 18? #DameBriony #KnightHerNow #BeLikeBriony

How many girls does it take to kill a predator? ONE #Hero #ILoveYouBriony #BeLikeBriony

We must protect this girl with everything we have #SheIsAGod-dess #BeLikeBriony

Superwoman #BeLikeBriony #PredatorsBeware #NotAfraid-Anymore

Got catcalled in the street. Turned and told him to repeat it again. Put my hands on his throat. He shat himself #BeLikeBriony #IHaveThePower

CHAPTER NINE

Briony was given a sick note for two weeks, which confused her as she wasn't sick, and whilst most teenagers would covet such a note, Briony was more concerned about how much schoolwork she would miss. She had a biology test she'd been revising for, and they were due to read Romeo and Juliet in English, and they were learning about the English Civil War in History—and she did not wish to miss out.

It was a relief, then, when Mum arrived in Briony's bedroom the morning after she'd arrived home following 'the incident' (this is how her mum referred to it) with piles of papers from her school that she'd just finished printing off.

"Right," she said, placing the pile on her desk. "I have emailed all of your teachers for work that you can catch up on, and they have all emailed me something, and I have printed it out for you, and here it is." She tilted her head at Briony. "But don't feel you must do it—it's just there if you want to. I completely understand if you wish to rest and recover, but if you want it, it's there, and I can help you with it if you want, or not, I don't know, it's up to you."

This was strange.

She was used to witnessing this reaction from her mum, but not toward her. Usually this occurred after one of Shane's suspensions from school—Mum would enter his room in the morning and dump a pile of papers on his desk with the instruction to catch up on work while he wasn't allowed in school. She'd offer to help him, and he'd either bark at her or ignore her, and she'd scuttle away to prepare his breakfast.

But today it was Briony who had breakfast prepared for her.

Her mother rushed out of the room and returned twenty minutes later with a tray. There was a glass of freshly squeezed orange juice, a freshly brewed coffee, a knife and fork, and a plate with poached eggs, bacon, sausages, and fried tomatoes.

"Now don't feel you have to eat it all," she said, placing the tray over Briony's legs as she sat up. "I wasn't sure if you'd be hungry or not, but it's all there, I won't be offended if you leave it, you just eat what you can. Can I get you anything else?"

Briony went to say no, then her mum interrupted her with an abrupt, "Oh, wait!"

She rushed out of the room and returned minutes later, struggling under the weight of the flat screen television they usually kept in the spare room for her dad to watch sports on.

"Do you want any help?" Briony said, looking for a way to move the breakfast off her lap.

"No!" Mum responded quickly as she placed the television on a chest of drawers. "You stay there and have your breakfast —I'll get this ready for you."

Within minutes, Briony had a perfect HD image of a morning chat show where a bunch of angry people were arguing over who the father was to one of their babies.

Mum sighed, smiled, and turned contentedly toward her daughter.

"Is there anything I'm forgetting?" she asked.

"Honestly, Mum, I'm fine."

"No, it's okay, I am not going anywhere—I have taken the week off work and I am here to help you in whatever way you can."

"That's nice, Mum, but–"

"No, I don't want to hear it! I am here to help you. Now, is there anything else you want?"

"No, I'm fine."

"You just give me a shout if you do," she said. "I'm just going to pop in the shower, then I'll come back to check on you."

She walked to the door, paused like she was forgetting something, then returned to the bed to plant a kiss on Briony's forehead before finally allowing herself to leave. Briony watched her go, looked at her breakfast, then to the television, then thought... *This is nice.*

She'd insisted that she was fine, that she didn't need doting upon, that she didn't need caring for—but honestly, she liked it. She hadn't had this much attention from her mum before. She could hear Shane stomping around downstairs, deliberately slamming the kitchen drawers and cupboards as he made his own breakfast, but she didn't care—it was finally her turn to have their mother's attention.

Over the next two weeks, things continued in the same way. Mum brought her breakfast, offered to help her with schoolwork, then spent all afternoon on the bed beside Briony, watching trashy television programs. They laughed at sitcoms, took the mickey out of awful Channel 5 movies, and debated over the issues brought up in pointless daytime talk shows.

When Briony started to feel restless after being couped up inside, Mum offered to drive her anywhere she wanted. If she wanted to go for a walk, they could do that; if they wanted to go shopping, she'd buy Briony clothes; if they wanted to go for a meal, she could just say what type of food she wanted.

And they did all of it.

The zoo, the safari park, country walks. Clothes shopping, book shopping, dine-in-for-two shopping. Italian restaurant, Indian, Tapas.

The child psychologist came to visit a few times, but aside from that, it was just her and Mum spending the best few weeks together.

It made Briony quite sad when the two weeks ended, and it was time for her to return to school.

Her mum offered to ask for an extension to the sick note, to say she could use the rest of her holiday if she needed to, to insist that they could stay at home if that's what Briony wanted—but they both knew Briony had to return to normality at some point. She was a studious child, keen to do well, and she did not want to fall behind in her education.

Even so, she was thrilled when her mother insisted that she'd pick her up and take her for ice cream at the end of the day.

RETURN TO SCHOOL RISK ASSESSMENT FOR BRIONY SPECTOR

Description of activity being assessed:
Student returning to school after traumatic experience

Year groups covered:
All

Locations covered:
All

Date of assessment:
20/1/2023

Agreed by governing body:
Meeting of governors 21/1/2023

Shared with staff:
22/1/2023

Shared with local authority:
By email to health and safety department

Author:
Mrs Letisha Cornwell

Formal review process:
Weekly between safeguarding lead (Sue Bingham), headteacher (Letisha Cornwell) and counsellor (Adrienne McKinty).

Amendments / Actions:
N/A

Risk:
Effect of trauma unknown

Rating:
High

Actions:
LC to lead meeting of teachers to instruct them to be vigilant of changes and behaviour, and further reminders in follow up email. Staff to inform SB, LC or AM of potential issues.

By:
LC

Risk:
Reaction of other students during reintegration

Rating:
Med

Actions:
LC and SB to be present when Briony enters
lunch hall for the first time. They are to
observe and only intervene if the reaction
of her peers becomes concerning. Should
this be an issue, further discussion is to
be had about how to manage Briony's return.

By:
LC SB

Risk:
Triggers during sex education lessons

Rating:
Med

Actions:
Briony to have her counselling sessions
during PSHE lessons to avoid triggers.

By:
AM

Risk:
Potential PTSD symptoms such as hypervigi-
lance or confusion

Rating:
High

Actions:
LC to inform teachers of importance of
vigilance.

By:
LC

CHAPTER TEN

Briony had barely set foot through the school gates before she was hurried into a small room that was half office, half waiting room, and told to wait for her 'counsellor'.

She couldn't recall anyone telling her she would have to talk to another counsellor, and she wasn't keen on the idea, but she didn't want to cause a fuss, so she did as she was told. The headmistress, a middle-aged woman in an ill-fitting suit and too much lipstick, asked if there was anything they could get her while she waited, but Briony said no—yet she didn't leave. She stared at her with her head tilted to the side, her lips in an almost pout, gazing at Briony like she was a delicate flower squashed beneath a bomb. She kept repeating things like, "I hope you are okay," and, "I hope you know we are here to help you." Briony gave awkward smile after awkward smile, and was pleased when she finally left the room muttering, "You brave, brave girl," as she did.

Briony didn't think she was brave. She'd had a moment where she'd lost control, and she didn't consider it to be brave, nor courageous. Honestly, she'd expected to feel shame, but she didn't even feel that—if anything, she felt empty. And not numb-empty—she felt weightless. Like her insides had fallen out and she could float around. There was a burden that had been lifted; a fear of constant threat that no longer existed. Respite from a terror she never realised she lived under.

Puberty had hit the boys in her classes over the last few years and had brought with it a huge sense of sexual entitlement. It had started with the boy behind her in Geography unhooking her bra, then it had been a boy trying to look up her skirt when she walked up the stairs, then it had been a boy who put her pencil case on his crotch and told her she could take it back whenever she wanted.

She didn't fear those boys anymore.

She'd previously felt a constant anxiety over their presence, like a persistent nausea, an awareness that they had the power to hurt her whenever they wanted—but now these boys seemed insignificant. The power had shifted, and they were no longer something to fear—she was now the one to be feared.

And whilst everyone predicted that she'd feel bad, or remorseful, or traumatised, or conflicted, or overwhelmed, none of them predicted the way she actually felt—which was *relief.*

A nearby door opened, and a small, mole-like woman poked her head out and smiled at Briony. She was short and her glasses seemed stuck on the end of her nose, causing her to have to lift her head back to see Briony clearly. She wore a denim dress with purple tights, and carried a notepad and one of those clicky pens that changes colour. She invited Briony into the room, sat opposite her, and produced the same sympathetic smile everyone wore in her presence.

"Briony," the woman said, her voice quiet and patronising like she was addressing a class of infants. "It is lovely to meet you, though I'm sad it must be under these circumstances. My name is Adrienne. How are you feeling today?"

Adrienne watched Briony expectantly, and Briony waited

for Adrienne to say something else. When no further conversation was forthcoming, Briony answered the question with a noncommittal shrug, eager to make this interaction as short as possible.

"I understand you've spoken to the child psychologist a few times, and she's said you're doing quite well. I am not here to force you to say anything you don't want to, but I am here to listen if you do. I am not a teacher, or your mother—I am a friend. Is that okay with you? If I'm a friend?"

Briony frowned. She can't remember saying that she wanted a friend.

"You are going to return to school life today, and it will be a difficult time for you, won't it? I am here for you anytime you need, if that's okay? You will have a timeout card, which means you can leave a lesson and come to me if things get too much, is that all right?"

Why did this woman keep asking if everything was all right? Briony hardly felt like she had much choice in the matter.

"Briony, is that all right?" Adrienne repeated, her voice becoming even more irritating with every question. Her tone was condescending in a way that Briony couldn't quite explain.

"Fine," Briony said.

"Ah, it's lovely to finally hear your voice! Well, I'm glad you are letting me be your friend. How are you feeling about coming back to school today?"

That same expectant look again. It lingered too long, like she would hold it until she received an answer, and Briony had no choice but to give it.

"Fine."

"Are you really, though? I mean, I would be surprised if you were."

"I mean, I've enjoyed staying at home and watching television. It's been pretty cool."

"I bet—is your television room your safe space?"

Briony frowned again. What the fuck is a safe space?

"Well, it's good to have them," Adrienne continued, as if she already knew the answer. "So you're feeling a bit nervous about it, then?"

"About what?"

"Coming back to school."

"No, not really."

"Do you want to come to school?"

"Yes."

Adrienne nodded like she'd just gained some valuable insight. Briony couldn't understand why. She'd always enjoyed learning, so why wouldn't she want to go to school?

"You are very brave, Briony. Very, very brave. But between these walls, when it's just you and I, you don't have to be brave. You can say how you are feeling. There will be no judgement from me, you understand?"

"Fine," Briony said, because she had to. Honestly, she couldn't care less about whether this woman judged her. She just wanted this to be over.

"Do you have any nightmares, Briony?"

The question stumped Briony; it seemed to come out of nowhere.

"No."

"What do you dream about?"

"I don't really remember."

"You block it out, do you?"

"Block what out?"

"Your dreams."

"No, I just don't remember them."

Adrienne nodded and wrote something down. What on earth could she be writing?

"It sounds like you're in denial, Briony."

"What's that?"

Adrienne sighed. "When we like to pretend we aren't feeling a certain way. How are you really feeling?"

Briony shrugged. "Bored."

"Bored? Are you finding being at home too boring?"

"No, I like being at home."

"So what is it you are finding boring?"

"What?"

Briony was confused. She found this boring, was that not clear?

"Right, well, I won't hold you back, I know you'll want to get to class and get it out of the way. Is there anything you'd like to share with me before you start your day?"

Why are you so mind-numbingly irritating?

"No."

"It will hit you, Briony. Eventually. It will all hit you, and it will become clear, and when that moment happens, just know you can come to me. Just use your pass and come to this room, okay?"

What was going to hit her? Briony didn't understand. She nodded along anyway, if only to make this meeting go by quicker.

"Good," Adrienne said. "I'm glad we had this chat. It's been lovely to meet you. Just remember, I'm here if you need me."

That expectant look again. Briony answered, "Fine."

And at last she was released, ready to return to the world of education and hormonal angst.

COUNSELLOR REPORT

Name:
Briony Spector

Birthdate:
5th October 2007

Age:
18

School year:
11

School:
Sandwell High School

Examiner:
Adrienne McKinty (Counsellor)

Referral Questions:
What is Briony's mental state? Is she going

to pose a risk to other students? Are other students going to pose a risk to her? How will she handle her reintegration? What is her current trauma response?

Assessment Procedure:
Briony is to have one-on-one sessions with me, beginning with before her re-entry, and ongoing sessions on a weekly basis, with extra sessions if needed. We have also asked teachers to be vigilant and observe her behaviour in class. The headmistress and I will observe her reintegration during lunch without making our presence known.

Report:
Briony was reluctant to talk or engage with me at first. This didn't seem to be because of apathy or a lack of interest—rather, she struggled to understand why she was meeting with me and gave little importance to what she had been through. The conversation was brief, and Briony appeared reluctant to engage with me, giving shorter answers. She stated she was not nervous about returning to school, though I wonder whether this might change once she resumes school life. It is my belief that she is yet to fully confront what she has been through. The school should be ready to react promptly should the trauma manifest during her reintegration, or if there are any triggers brought on by conversations with peers or teachers. For now, she seems in sound mind,

though I feel this is because she doesn't fully realise what has happened to her. I recommend close observation.

CHAPTER ELEVEN

D ue to the counselling and being made to wait around, Briony did not return to school until break time. She expected to enter the canteen and remain unnoticed, like she always had been, and did not expect the entire student body to stop eating, rise to their feet, and applaud her.

But this was what happened.

She stood in the doorway, astonished, bemused and discomforted by the attention—at first, anyway—but the longer the applause went on, the more it delighted her. She smiled and gushed and fiddled with her fingers and looked away and back again, but the applause didn't stop. It went on. And it wasn't just the students—the staff table, and the dinner ladies, and even the bloke mending a faulty projector all stood and bashed their hands together.

When the applause eventually died down, a group of girls ushered her over. This was a group of girls who had never looked her way before, yet seemed keen to welcome her now. The boys stared at her, and the other tables looked annoyed that these girls had claimed her first. Briony fiddled with her hair and shuffled to the table where they all slid across so she could fit on the bench.

Briony did not know what to say to these girls, but she needn't have worried as they didn't give her much opportunity to talk—they were all desperate to declare their admiration for her: "Oh you were so brave," "I wish I could do that to a boy," "How did it feel?" "How did you have the courage?" "I have a boy who won't leave me alone, what do you think I should do?"

As ignored as she had been before, was as praised and sought after and included as she was now. Friendship swarmed at her from all angles in all lessons and all break times and all lunches; boys who wanted the filthy details; teachers who wished to protect her; grim stoners who loved anything violent and twisted—but it was in these girls who had previously snubbed her where she found her tribe; girls who'd been harassed and touched and objectified by their male peers who saw her actions as empowering.

Girls who felt they didn't have to take that shit anymore.

It had been constant, the way the boys had treated them: boys who gave them ratings from one to ten; boys who called them frigid when they withdrew their consent at a drunken party; boys who stroked their bum as they passed in the corridor, then claimed they were making it up; boys who flapped their tongue at them from across the classroom; boys who peered up skirts; boys who sent unsolicited dick pics; boys who put an unwanted hand on a girl's leg under the desk; and boys who ridiculed any girl who objected to any of these things by labelling them as hysterical.

But not anymore.

So long as Briony was part of their group, these girls were exempt from harassment.

These boys knew what she had done to a man—a man who was what these boys seemed destined to become—and they were terrified to cross her.

Briony was still a quiet person, and spent most of her time with these girls in silence, smiling at the conversation and the admiration—but she was no longer silent like a victim. She was silent like the eye of the storm, or the stalk of a lioness, or the clenching of a fist.

She was the thing her friend's fears now feared.

And they welcomed her onto the girl's football team; the one thing she'd yearned for. Both her team and the opposition formed a guard of honour for her as she entered the pitch for their first game, and every spectator at the side of the pitch struck their hands together in rapturous applause as she took to the field.

Her teammates passed her the ball at every opportunity, and she always found a teammate in a good position with a succinct pass—and even in those times she didn't, it didn't matter. They still patted her on the back and told her it was a good try, to keep going, she was doing great.

After the game, the headmistress informed her that the local MP wished to present her with an award for bravery, and would do so in their next assembly. It would be a certificate of recognition for having the courage to stand up for herself, to defend herself, to fight against a predator who should have known better.

Briony said that she wasn't bothered about the award, but it was nice to be acknowledged. To be noticed. To be in someone's thoughts.

Of course, it would be natural for you to wonder how her trauma might eventually manifest—she had been through a horrific experience, after all. But there were no flashbacks, no meltdowns, no anxiety, no nightmares, no insomnia—all those things may yet come, but for now, they only existed in speculation. She had become possessed for a moment and did what she must to survive. It had not been a courageous or admirable act, but a necessary one—yet she was beginning to learn that it was courageous, and that it was admirable. That she was being commended and rewarded for inflicting violence on her assailant.

She was learning that when she killed an older man in a hotel room, she became wonderful.

She was noticed.

She was present.

But there was one thing left inside of her, something burning but not yet alight, something that glowed but remained temporarily dim.

She didn't understand it yet, but she soon would.

It was Rage.

But to say that she was full of Rage would be to give too little credit to Rage.

She wasn't 'full' of Rage.

She *was* Rage.

She was the reason the word held so much power.

It was her that Rage was created for.

And as anyone who ever feels such insurmountable Rage will attest to—eventually that Rage needs an outlet.

For now, she was content with being seen, in being recognised. She was happy to be in people's thoughts, and she was rewarded every day for the Rage she'd previously enacted.

You see, it wasn't her actions that she thought were being rewarded—it was Rage. And, being Rage personified, it was *she* that was the glorious act of violence the world was rewarding.

She was the bomb that was yet to explode, and when the constant rewards ended, she'd only need a match to light the fuse; then that bomb would explode, and it would be magnificent—Rage would rain upon us, and we would finally know what a girl without limits can do.

TRANSCRIPT OF TELEPHONE CONVERSATION BETWEEN BEATRICE SPECTOR AND DCI KEVIN MCCLUSKEY

Beatrice

Kevin (…) I (…) I'm speaking to you as a family friend not (…) not as a police officer though I know that's (…) that's the official line (…) but that's not (…) not how this is (…) I (…) I don't even know…

Kevin

Beatrice (…) why don't you tell me what's troubling you.

Beatrice

It's Briony she (…) she's been through so much (…) she's still so young and she suddenly seems so grown up and I (…) it just feels like (…) I've heard about survivors (…) read stuff (…) there was an article I found on Google that said how girls with trauma from rape tend to act grown up (…) make up (…) sexual conversation (…) suddenly they act beyond their age.

Kevin

She is eighteen Beatrice (…) make up and sexual conversation isn't that far from what we might expect.

Beatrice

I know it's just (…) it doesn't feel right.

Kevin

What is it that doesn't feel right?

Beatrice

She's slipping away from me (…) every day she seems angry (…) not in conversation with her I talk to her and she's fine it's not that it's (…) sometimes I look at her when she's not talking to anyone or when she's got a book in front of her or watching TV and she (…) she's (…) frowning kind of grimacing (…) like she's glaring at something that isn't there.

Kevin

She's angry.

Beatrice

Yes (…) but I don't ever see it (…) not overtly I mean.

Kevin

What is it you're worried about?

Beatrice

That she might (…) I don't know (…) I don't think she'd ever harm herself I just (…) I don't know.

Kevin

Do you worry she might harm someone else?

Beatrice

God no (…) she's a sweet girl (…) before this happened she was I (…) I don't know what she is now (…) god I can't believe I just said that.

Kevin

It's okay (…) I know this is all about Briony (…) but you also have things that you're feeling too after all it (…) it is your daughter that's been through this (…) she was raped Beatrice and you're bound to feel guilty.

Beatrice

But she wasn't just raped was she I (…) I don't mean *just* raped I'm not really saying this right I (…) I mean she defended herself didn't she?

Kevin

She certainly did.

Beatrice

Kevin (…) she killed a man (…) what does that do to a person (…) a young girl.

Kevin

A young woman.

Beatrice

She's eighteen.

Kevin

You'd be surprised what I find eighteen-year-olds doing in my line of work.

Beatrice

Yes but those are bad eighteen year (…) I mean not bad (…) they aren't Briony (…) god you must think I'm an awful person.

Kevin

Not at all (…) I think you're struggling and it's not surprising considering what your family is going through.

Beatrice

What would you do (…) I mean if you (…) you were in my position (…) what would you do?

Kevin

I'd give her space (…) don't crowd her (…) don't over mother her (…) let her work this out and she will come to you in time (…) she knows you're there for her (…) give her love but don't cling to her.

Beatrice

But I (…) I want to protect her so much.

Kevin

And that may lead to you protecting her too much.

Beatrice

So I should stop (…) what (…) mothering her?

Kevin

You should never stop mothering your child (…) just make sure you're not being too much for her (…) focus on your son as well (…) he needs you too.

Beatrice

Okay.

Kevin

She'll be all right (…) she will.

Beatrice

Are you sure?

Kevin

As sure as I can be.

Beatrice

Thank you Kevin (…) thank you (…) I appreciate it (…) I'm glad I called.

Kevin

If you need me to talk to her (…) to help (…) I can take her for a walk and have a chat (…) it might help.

Beatrice

Maybe (…) if she needs it.

Kevin

Okay, Beatrice.

Beatrice

I better go.

Kevin

Talk to me any time.

Beatrice

I will (…) thank you (…) goodbye Kevin.

Kevin

Goodbye (…) and er (…) Beatrice (…) I miss you.

Beatrice

I know.

CHAPTER TWELVE

And so they presented her with her certificate for bravery.

It was in the main hall at school, and all her year group was there, her new friends sat on the front row, on the edge of their seats with their hands on their knees and their smiles spread too wide across their made-up faces.

She did what she was supposed to do. She walked onstage to the applause she was becoming used to, smiled routinely at the headmistress, and shook hands with the local politician. He was some smarmy middle-aged guy in a suit with parted hair and a voice stained by upper-class privilege. He made her stand there as he spoke into the small microphone at the top of the podium about enduring hard times, as if he knew what hard times even looked like.

"...and so we must find our own courage, just like a young woman such as Briony Spector did, such an admirable girl, for she has fought against the very thing that oppresses us..."

Briony wondered whether he'd even written the speech himself.

After a while, they prompted her to smile for the cameras,

and she dutifully obeyed—there were several of them, all gathered at the front, with their big lenses directed at her, flashes going off every few seconds. The politician (she didn't pay attention to his name) didn't react to the photographers—not even once. He didn't look at them or flinch at the bright flashing white lights—instead, he locked eyes with his audience, speaking in the way his expensive fancy private school would have taught him to, and with a confidence that sat upon him with the smear of entitlement.

"...for when we encourage such young women to act against their attackers, we encourage all young women to act against those who attack them in whatever form, and know that there are no real threats or dangers lurking on the street when you have a wise head on your shoulders..."

She wondered if he had any idea what it was like to be a woman in this world; perhaps he'd read an article on it, or perhaps he'd had a brief conversation with a feminist at a political event. He spoke about the dangers they faced with such a narrow understanding of what they were—as if the only threat a woman faces is a man in a dark alley wearing a balaclava who strips her and muzzles her mouth. He was completely unaware of the heckles of builders; the way a woman on a date texts her friends at pre-arranged times to let them know she's okay; the clutching of keys as she passes a stranger; the men who make comments; men who say *you're overreacting* to having her bum pinched in a nightclub, as if casual sexual assault isn't something to be upset by—she wondered if he had any idea what it was like to worry whether being alone with a man was a potential risk, or whether she'd be blamed for her rape because she invited the man to her bedroom.

"...women who know how to dress properly shouldn't have to put up with these kinds of men, especially not young women like Briony..."

Young women like Briony.

What exactly did that mean? What kind of young woman was Briony? Quiet? Withheld? Hard-working? Pretty? From a two-parent middle-class household? White?

She was the ideal victim. The paper's wet dream. The politician's perfect profile-booster.

"...and so I give you this certificate of bravery to show what a courageous young girl you are."

He handed over a certificate. An A3 piece of cardboard with sentimental writing in a cheap font and a printed signature at the bottom. He beamed at her like he'd just given her a million pounds.

"Thank you," she responded obediently.

She looked into the crowd and scrutinised the faces; the way her headmistress held back tears; the way her new friends doted on her with loyal, admiring stares; the way the boys folded their arms.

It all felt so... manufactured.

After another pointless spiel from the politician and another round of applause, it ended, and she left, and they kept on talking and she walked into the reception and she stopped. Looked down at the certificate. And she wanted to leave.

So she left.

She punched open the fire exit and marched out of the school and down the road—but stopped at about thirty yards or so, her good-girl instinct fighting her rebellion. She didn't know why she felt such an urge to run. She knew she shouldn't. She didn't truant school.

She compromised with herself—she'd have a few minutes on her own. To breathe. To clear her mind. To get away from the sycophants who adored her. Then she'd go back.

She ran her hands through her hair. Looked around. A woman leant against the railings that separated the pavement from the school's playing field. She glared at Briony with an intensity that alarmed her. Her skin was a faded dark pale, her clothes crumpled, her body drooping.

"Too much for you?" the woman asked. Her voice was gravelly and spiteful. It felt wrong.

Briony shot her a smile that she hoped would placate her.

It didn't.

"Disgusting, isn't it?" the woman continued. "Everyone sucking your dick like you're the best thing in the world. Like you did something other than brutally murder a man that *you* led on."

Now Briony was paying attention. She looked the woman up and down, scowling at her, clutching her certificate as if it was a weapon. The woman narrowed her eyes and spat a wad of phlegm into a puddle. She stood up off the fence, took a drag of her cigarette, stubbed it out, and stepped toward Briony.

Briony did not leave.

"Think I don't know?" the woman said, her voice low in a way that sounded sinister. "Think I didn't see the messages?"

"What messages?" Briony asked. Her voice sounded smaller than she intended.

"You sent him messages, you told him you loved him, you asked for him to tell you how special you are. And yet they are telling everyone that *you* are the victim." She scoffed.

"Who are you?" Briony asked, although it didn't take much to figure it out. She noticed the wedding ring that still clung to her bony fingers. The bags under her eyes from sleepless nights of staring at news article after news article on her phone screen. The way her teeth ground together with a fury Briony found too familiar.

She hadn't known that Adam—who she now knew was called Gordon—was married. But she knew now.

"He groomed me," Briony insisted.

"Hah!" The woman snatched the certificate from Briony's hands. "What is this shit? Certificate of bravery?"

Her face contorted into something unnatural—it could have been wrath, scorn, denial, defensiveness, self-preservation—or a sordid mixture of all five. Either way, there was something bubbling, and Briony knew it would not be good.

"I think I should leave now," Briony said, and went to take her certificate back.

The woman ripped the certificate. She stepped toward Briony and, despite being a foot smaller, seemed to grow bigger.

Briony disregarded the certificate and turned back toward to school. The woman's slimy fingers wrapped around her wrist and stopped Briony from being able to go.

"Let go of me!"

"Or what?"

"Let me go!"

She tried to pull her arm free, but this woman was holding too tight.

"Perhaps you shouldn't have been such a slut."

"Please!"

"Or a whore."

"Please stop!"

"And my husband would still be here right now!"

She finally pulled her arm free.

But she didn't run. Didn't leave. Didn't go.

She glared back at this woman.

This woman who had called her a slut. A whore. Who wished her assailant back to life.

And the Rage that has been referred to—that thing that Briony was made of—it came to the surface, and Briony was no longer in control.

The woman tried to grab Briony again, but she was slow, and tired, and still drunk, and she was on the floor with Briony on top of her before she could fight back—and no matter how much she waved and thrashed her arms, her weak limbs were nothing compared to the Rage that mounted her.

Rage was slow, Rage was particular, and Rage was well-thought out.

She placed her thumbs over the woman's eyelids.

She pushed down—gently, at first. Like a tease. Just foreplay.

Then she pushed harder.

It was like pressing thumbs against a sponge that was hard in the centre. Or pressing down on a peach and reaching the pip. The eyelids were soft, but the eyeballs were hard, and it took force to push them further and further into the woman's skull; she dug her fingernails into the woman's cheeks at the same time, bringing about beads of blood—and *that* was something she relished. It seeped over her fingers and dribbled down her skirt and decorated the pavement with Rage, Rage, Rage.

By the time they got to her, the woman's eyeballs had almost burst.

But it was okay.

Because they wrapped a blanket around Briony and apologised to her. Told her she shouldn't have had to face that; that the police had lost track of where the woman had ended up; that the school should have done something when they noticed her hanging around the school earlier, it was their fault really, all their fault.

That she did what she had to do in self-defence.

And those two hyphenated words—self-defence—became an excuse, then became a motivation, then became a prerogative.

They apologised for failing to protect her. The school. The politician. The police. Her friends. Her mother. They were all so, so sorry.

There was nothing Rage could do but soak up the regrets they piled upon her, and slowly learn that Rage was what they wanted.

When Briony awoke the next morning, she was happy, and

she did her teeth and put on her dress and went to school like she did every other day. Rage was gone.

But not forever.

She lay dormant. Waiting.

And Rage did not like to be kept waiting.

RIPPED CERTIFICATE OF BRAVERY

THIS IS

_____BR_____

HAS SHOWN EX

HONOUR IN T

SIGNED

o Cert

Spector

TIONAL BRAVERY

HE FACE OF ADVER

(The

THAT

D

YOR)

CHAPTER THIRTEEN

Another day, another crime scene.

It was his job. Kevin knew that. It was painfully reminded to him any time he mentioned it; he'd open up to a friend, only to be immediately shut down with a bemused, "Surely you knew what you were getting yourself into?"

He did know, in the sense that he knew it would be tough, that he knew he'd see things he couldn't unsee, and that he'd face horrible situations... But does anyone ever truly know what they are getting into?

Sure, people can tell you that you'll see a dead body, but no one can tell you that you'll see that same body over and over again in the faces of strangers, and that you'll never forget how scared their final expression was.

Sure, they can tell you that you'll get into scraps with scumbags—but no one can tell you what it's like to sit in a cell with one of these scumbags, your cheek still swollen from their punch, listening them break down over their drug addiction, and how much they wished they didn't have to go back to sleeping on the street once you released them.

Sure, survivors of domestic abuse can tell you how important it is to have officers that understand—but they can never tell you how much it hurts to drop charges against a prolific abuser because the victim has gone back to them.

They can tell you about the things you'll see and do, but they could never tell you about the experience of seeing and doing them.

It hadn't always bothered him. He used to convince himself that he was making a difference, and that made it worthwhile. But all he did nowadays was show up to crime scenes and give orders.

As he drove around another corner with a sigh, something in a nearby car park caught his attention. He slowed down. A scruffy teenage boy was standing over a kid, shouting in his face.

Kevin recognised the scruffy teenage boy, but couldn't quite place him.

He pulled his car to the side of the road and stepped out. The kid on the floor saw Kevin first and legged it. The teenage boy, however, saw Kevin too late and, by the time he turned to run, Kevin was already at his side with a hand on his arm.

"Get the fuck off me!" the teenager shouted. "Don't fucking touch me!"

His face was so familiar, but Kevin had dealt with many wayward teenage boys in his job, and it was hard to separate them from each other.

Then Kevin realised where he recognised this boy.

It was from the case he could never forget.

Briony Spector—the girl who valiantly fought off her attacker in a hotel room. This was her older brother. Beatrice's son.

"Shane," Kevin said, as much to himself as to the boy. "Shane Spector?"

"What?" Shane grunted. There wasn't even a smidgeon of

respect for Kevin's authority—Shane was hostile and ready to kick off.

Kevin considered whether this was worth it. He had a boot full of evidence that needed to be processed, and an arrest now would add even more to his already excessive workload. He didn't have time for this.

Yet he felt something for the girl's family. A deep empathy, perhaps. And he wanted to help.

"If I let go of you, and you run off, I'm nicking you on the spot, understood?" Kevin said.

"Fine."

Kevin released Shane's arm. Shane brushed himself off, then turned back to Kevin with a sneer, and waited to hear what Kevin wanted.

But what did he want?

What was the point of this?

"Look," Kevin said, attempting to improvise. "What the hell are you doing?"

"What?"

"The kid you were beating on."

"He was trying to nick my sweets."

"Nick your sweets…" Kevin shook his head. What a petty thing to prompt such aggression.

"Yeah, and? Didn't want a beating, he shouldn't have tried nicking my sweets."

"Why aren't you in school, anyway?"

"I'm suspended."

"Why?"

"They said I was fighting."

Kevin tried to lead Shane to a nearby bench. "Come on, let's have a sit down."

"Nah, I'm all right."

Kevin stared at Shane, and saw in his face a familiar expression—one he'd seen in thousands of delinquents over the past three decades. It made him feel tired. Weary. Old. The only thing that changed was the name; the anger in these kids was always the same. The same strut, the same scowl, the same attitude, like the world owed them something.

"Look, I get it," Shane said. "You want to be the big bollocks and try to change my life and all that—you piggies are all the same. I don't want some inspirational talk. There's nothing you can say that's going to change me."

"And what about your family? What about your sister and all she's been through?"

Shane snorted, and his expression contorted into something between a smile and a scowl. "My sister ain't all she's cracked up to be."

"Excuse me?"

"I said she ain't the saint you think she is."

Kevin wasn't sure what to say—if there even was anything to say. He sighed, then concluded, "Go home, Shane. Or I will nick you."

"Fine. We done?"

Kevin nodded. Shane shoved his hands in his pockets and strode across the car park. Kevin watched him go until he was out of sight.

He knew he should dismiss Shane's comments and put them down to words of a disgruntled older brother, or a troubled teen, or an angry boy. But there was something about them that made him think…

Was there more to Briony's story?

No. He shook his head. The girl was eighteen.

She did what she had to do.

He returned to his car and took the evidence to the station. Once it was processed, he set up an incident room and assigned tasks to the officers involved—collecting CCTV, getting statements, that kind of thing. Then, when it was only an hour after his shift was supposed to end, he gave Shane's mother a call. Let her know what had happened. Advised her to talk to her son.

He hoped she would talk to him with the patience he was sure she was capable of.

CHAPTER FOURTEEN

They say that time is a great healer and that we all move on eventually.

And this, inevitably, was what happened over the next few months.

It started on a hot Wednesday evening. The garden doors were open, allowing a deep humidity to sneak through the house, and Briony and her family were in shorts and t-shirts. She sat on the sofa, watching television, with the noise of an argument between Shane and Mum coming from upstairs. Dad sat next to her, not getting involved—he generally went to work then came back and sat on the sofa, only having small conversations with his children. It was Mum who was the hub of the house, and whatever Shane had done, it had riled her up.

Briony ignored it. Watched the show about gardens being made over, with her certificate hung in a frame on the near wall. Mum had reattached the pieces of certificate in a way that was hugely noticeable; a mixture of glue and Sellotape haphazardly applied. Briony wasn't that bothered about it, but Mum was, and this had made Briony smile—that Mum wanted to show off her daughter's achievements, and her awards, and her bravery, was something that Briony relished.

Especially after the day she'd had.

She'd gone to speak to the headmistress, who'd said her door was open for Briony at any time only a few weeks ago, just to ask if she was coming to the next football game. But the door was not open to her this time, and the headmistress had another student in her office. She'd hurriedly asked Briony, "Is it important, or can it wait?"

Briony had answered delicately, "It can wait."

And the door had been closed with no further comment.

She'd gone to find her friends in the canteen; her friends who always saved her a seat and welcomed her into their conversation. Only this time, they had left the canteen without her, and when she found them outside, none of them acknowledged her arrival. When they left for their lesson, no one stopped to see if Briony was coming, or if she'd done the homework, or if she was dreading another hour of geography; they just left, leaving her sitting on the grass without an invitation.

She'd gone to her football match, searched for her name on the team sheet, and found it on the bench. At first she figured, fine, they probably wanted to bring her on as an impact sub, and when they were a goal down with half an hour to go, and the coach looked at Briony, she expected to go on.

But the coach asked the girl sat next to Briony instead.

And Briony didn't go on. They came back to win 2-1, and they celebrated without her. Briony didn't run onto the pitch at the final whistle with the other substitutes, and no one involved her in the singing in the changing room afterwards, and no one asked if her she was going to the afterparty.

Briony had been a fad.

Like Tamagotchis or flared jeans or yoyos or braids in your hair or the Macarena; she was the big thing one day, and then suddenly... she was forgotten. She returned to the absent presence she had been before, strolling through the hallway unnoticed, and no longer cared for.

She wasn't worth talking about anymore.

Her story was impressive at the time, but it was done now. There was fresh news. A girl in their year was pregnant, and two boys had a fight that meant one of them lost three teeth, and a teacher quit because of inappropriate comments to students. She fell down the list of exciting recent events until she dropped off it completely. Her time had passed, and she was no longer the hot topic being discussed.

She figured it didn't matter; she still had Mum and her new levels of affection, and that was most important—but as soon as Briony returned home from school, ready for some time with her mother, Shane had stomped down the stairs with his fists curled and his nose snarled and his stomps heavy, and Mum came charging after him, matching his temper.

"And I'm supposed to take another day off work because you got suspended again?"

"I never asked you to, I'm old enough to be at home on my own!"

"I wouldn't trust you at home on your own, you'd wreck it."

"Well maybe I'll find a new home!"

"Where? Who's going to take you?"

"Anywhere but here would be good!"

"All this because you can't avoid throwing your fists at the first sign of anger?"

"He pissed me off!"

"Everyone pisses you off, Shane, it's not new! You think you aren't pissing me off right now?"

"I don't care!"

"But I'm not swinging my fist because you're pissing me off. I'm trying to talk to you!"

"Oh yeah, this really sounds like talking."

"Guys…" Dad stood and held out a calming hand, as if he had any authority. Shane glared at him, snorting like a bull, then turned to Briony, his eyes leering at his sister for no other reason than because she was there.

"Look at Briony," Mum continued. "She never gets suspended, never gets in fights!"

"What, but her killing a bloke is fine?"

"That's not the same!"

"No, it's worse! I punched a kid who called me a faggot, she killed a fucking man!"

"Do not swear at me, Shane!"

"Is that all you take from what I just said?"

"For Christ's sake, Shane!" She lowered her voice to a calm wobble and she said clearly and articulately, "Why can't you be more like your sister?"

The shouting stopped, but the tension grew louder. Shane's glare grew more intense. His head shook with increasing vehemence. His breath grew quicker. His fury was something his body couldn't contain.

Mum seemed to realise what she just said, and began, "Shane, I–"

Then Shane did something he knew he could not come back from.

He pulled his fist back and launched it at the framed certificate, smashing it into several shards of glass that collided with the floor.

Briony wasn't bothered, but Mum dove to her knees and collected the shards in her arms, shaking and quivering.

Shane stood back, growing vaguely aware of what he'd done.

"How dare you…" Mum's voice was small and croaky. She turned her gaze past Shane and focussed her stare on Briony. "We'll get you a new frame. We will, I promise."

"Sorry, Br–" Shane began, but Mum was on her feet and

jabbing a finger in his face before he could finish his sister's name.

"How dare you! You do not talk to her! If you had any idea what she'd been through, if you had any kind of empathy, then you would know that there is no apologising."

He stormed out of the room. Mum followed, the pieces of frame still in her arms.

Briony didn't see them for the rest of the night—but she sure heard them. There was no escape. No matter how long she laid in bed, waiting for it to end so she could sleep, the roars of battle shook the floor and the walls.

The next morning, Mum kept insisting she'd get a new frame. That she'd find one soon. That she'd put the certificate back up.

Shane didn't say a word. He just walked in and ate his breakfast and returned to his room.

Over the next few weeks, he demanded more and more attention, just like before. There were no more cuddles in front of the television, no more heartfelt conversations on the way to school, no more mother and daughter afternoons. Shane's insubordination once again occupied Mum's time. He returned to school a week later and was suspended again shortly after, this time for something he said to a teacher— Briony didn't keep track of the reasons. She just kept track of how it felt, sitting all alone, the invisible girl in a house full of people.

She sank further into the background, knowing there was only one thing that got her noticed. That made her mum care. That forced her friends to pay attention.

Rage sat idly by, waiting for her moment.

Briony held Rage's hand and promised her time would come soon.

Mum never did buy a new photo frame.

EXCERPT FROM CONVERSATION ON PUBLIC CHATROOM 'TEEN CHAT SOCIAL'

Hi

Hello there

What's your name?

Charlie
What's yours?

I'm Briony
I saw your post
I saw you were wanting to chat

I am

How come?

I'm bored I guess
Just wanted some female company

Fair enuf

How old are you?

I'm 18
How old are you

I'm in my forties

That's a lot older than me

Is that a problem?

Nah
Is it 4 u?

I don't mind if you don't mind
So long as you're comfortable
I don't want you to think I'm pressuring you

Pressuring me into what?
Talking?

Sure

If you were pressuring me I cud just close the conversation
Use that big X in the corner
U aren't pressuring me
I don't need to be pressured

I'm sure you don't
I'm sorry if you thought I was being rude

Y r u wantin to talk to a 18 year old anyway?

I can relate better
Everyone my age is so dull

PERVERTED LITTLE FREAK

Do you know what I mean?

Yeh
My dad just sits on the sofa all day watching tv
He is so boring

See, that is boring
But I'm not boring like that
I like doing things

Like what things

Going out for walks
Going to the cinema
Taking drives
Just hanging out
Do you like those things?

I guess

It seems like we have a lot in common

All apart from our age lol

Age is just a number
It doesn't matter
I don't know why people make such a big deal out of it

I dunno
I guess some people find it gross

Urgh
People can be so judgemental
Don't you think?

Yer

That's why I don't listen to people
Or even tell them that I'm on here
They aren't like you
They don't understand
They aren't special

U think im special?

Yes

Uve only been talkin to me for like 2 mins

I know
But I can tell
I don't need to know someone for hours, I can just tell
Do you know what I mean?

I guess

Do you think I'm special?

I dunno lol

Maybe it's too soon
But in time maybe you will

Yer
Crap my mums calling me
I g2go now anyway

Well it's been really nice talking to you Briony
Perhaps we can chat again sometime?

Sure
I'll be on again tomorrow night

Same time?

About the same time

I look forward to talking to you again

Me too

Or if you want
You could give me your number
Then we can text instead of being on here
And we can talk whenever

Sure its [NUMBER REDACTED]
Maybe we cn even meet sometime
I dno
Nyway
g2g
bye

Goodbye Briony

Goodbye Charlie

xxxx

CHAPTER FIFTEEN

Rat-Face-Counsellor-Lady—or Adrienne, as she insisted on being called—sat in the same armchair with the same clipboard and the same pen and the same denim dress and the same purple tights, gazing at Briony in a poor attempt to look pensive. Her chair wasn't big, but it still made her look very small.

Briony had hated these counselling sessions; of feeling constantly observed, constantly judged; of persistently being asked stupid questions, then being forced to fill the silence. She was fed up with the look this woman had when she spoke, like she was waiting for Briony to fall apart, like Briony was a delicate petal who might float away from her wilted stem should the rain fall too hard. She did not need help—she was not weak. She was powerful. She had killed a man twice her weight, and she did not need some condescending bitch talking down to her in sessions that were tedious and monotonous and pointless—she was capable of things this woman could not conceive of, and it was an insult that she thought she could help Briony.

Even so, Briony had enjoyed the attention.

She had felt special that the school thought she was worth the time.

"Well," Adrienne-Rat-Face-Counsellor-Lady said, putting her clipboard to the side and placing her hands on her knees like she was a primary school teacher about to give instructions to an infant. "This will be the last time you'll see me."

Briony frowned. "Where are you going?"

"I'm not going anywhere." She chuckled. Briony hated that she chuckled. "I'll still be in this same office, I'll just be sat with other students, talking about other things."

Briony felt oddly betrayed, like this was a lover breaking up with her then bragging about all the future lovers they were going to have. She wanted the sessions to end, but she didn't want to accept that the school no longer believed she was worth the time.

"Am I done?" Briony asked.

"I think so. I'm not sure there's anything else you'll get from these sessions. Do you?"

Briony shrugged. She didn't want to admit that she felt an unexpected sadness that they were ending. So she remained silent.

"I think that's my answer," Adrienne said, and stood up, though it didn't make her much taller.

"So what now?" Briony asked, not standing up.

"Now, you return to lessons. Keep going. Life goes on as normal. That's the strange thing about traumatic experiences, you expect them to stay forever, then you find it's been weeks and they are very much in the past."

Adrienne held open the door and raised her eyebrows at Briony. Briony knew she was meant to stand up and exit through it, she just felt... Hesitant. Mum's attention turned back to Shane, her supposed friends' attention had turned back to each other, and now this infuriating woman's attention was ending.

People didn't care about her any longer.

She wasn't interesting enough.

The day of her uniqueness had ended, and she was to resume being the same empty face unnoticed in a busy corridor just as she had been before.

She stood, picked up her bag, marched to the door, then halted in the doorway. She turned back to Adrienne and glared at her mole-like features. Her glasses took up most of her face.

"Your spectacles are stupid," Briony said, and she left, not looking back. She was sure Adrienne was watching her, confused, and Briony wasn't too sure why she'd said it, but she didn't care. She just walked, as fast as she could without jogging, and turned the corner.

She entered her fifth period classroom—a science laboratory. She awaited her teacher's greeting and her peer's questions of where she'd been, but no one even noticed her walking in. The teacher sat at the desk, absorbed in their screen, and the students looked down at their exercise books, answering questions from a textbook. She walked between two aisles of students, and none of them even flinched.

She took a seat at the back of the class and waited. For someone to acknowledge her, perhaps, or for someone to tell her what work she was doing. But no interaction came. She was a fly that had floated in and landed where she would bother people the least.

She took out her phone and held it beneath the desk. Several of the men she was talking to the previous night had replied. A few had stopped talking when she revealed her age. Another few had stopped when she said she wanted to meet, no strings attached—possibly presuming she was too good to be true, and they were going to get caught. But there were a few still replying.

Most were not afraid to share their age. One in his twenties. One in his thirties. A few in their forties, and the odd one in retirement. They all agreed to meet. Some said they just wanted to talk, some said they wanted to fuck her, and some had already sent her a stream of dick pics; most of which resembled slugs.

She chose the men who seemed the nicest—because they were the ones who hid it the best—and she kept talking to them. She was like a judge on her favourite talent show, selecting from the auditionees, then putting them on stage to be scrutinised. Some would make it, some wouldn't—but whoever won the final would have the grandest prize of all.

She saw these men like David saw Goliath; like the tortoise saw the hare; like Medusa saw stone—and these men saw her as a single rose that fell out of the bouquet, discarded on the floor to be trampled on; only unique because she was no longer protected by thorns. It was her innocence they wanted the most. The inherent naivety that clung to her messages. The harmless question of what they meant. Like the one who said he wanted to wreck her. What exactly was there to wreck?

The more she didn't know, the more they loved it.

There was something she did to these men they struggled to deny. She could draw them in with such ease, like it was natural—but it wasn't natural, it was horrid, and most men would feel immense shame over the sordid thoughts she'd conjure within them.

And I emphasise—*most* men.

Because there were always some men willing to risk the life they'd had built just to satisfy their dicks for a single minute.

But don't worry, dick-led men.

Don't you worry at all.

Briony will not need the entire minute.

TEXT MESSAGES RETRIVED FROM BRIONY SPECTOR'S PHONE

I'm really enjoying talking to you this evening Briony

You seem like a really nice girl

I'm grateful that you've opened up to me

It sounds like your parents are quite tough to live with

I only wish I could help

Me too

Maybe you could whisk me away somewhere

We could run away together lol

I'd like that

I was jokin

I wasn't

You really want to run away?

Where would we go?

France

Spain

Africa

Who cares

Somewhere we can be free

Wouldn't it be weird for you to be hanging out with a 18yrold?

In Nigeria the age of consent is 11

We could go there

No one would think we're weird there

The problem is the place we live in, not how we feel

I don't know if I want to live in Nigeria

There's plenty of places that will accept us Briony

We can find somewhere

And we can live there forever

Would you like that?

Sure

Maybe we should meet first

Maybe go for a walk in the park

Feed the ducks

Spend a bit of time together

Why don't we just go to a hotel

Skip the park

Really?

Are you sure?

Yes

Let's just book a room

And what would you like to do in that room?

:P

You are full of surprises

You have no idea

CHAPTER SIXTEEN

There weren't many benefits to having a stressed-out mother with major issues with insomnia—the tired rants and frequent tempers and raised voices toward Shane were all exacerbated by such issues—but the prescription drugs left in the cabinet were pretty useful on this occasion.

Briony took a few pills from each packet, ensuring that they wouldn't be noticeably depleted in quantity, and smashed each pill into powder on a piece of paper. She didn't recognise the names—limbitrol, Valium, xanax, temazepam, lorazepam, clonazepam (there seemed to be a lot of 'zepams')—but she hoped that, all mixed together, they would make a sedative with the power she needed. She poured the contents into a syringe, added a little water to make it thicker, then put it in her leather satchel along with her other items.

She got on the bus with no concerns. Gone was the shy girl, terrified to get off at the wrong stop; here was the strong, confident young woman who had the correct change ready, and the stop memorised.

He said his name was Charles. That he was 42 but felt

younger. That he'd be wearing a blue shirt and jeans. She hadn't expected, however, to see such a nerdy man with his shirt tucked tightly into those jeans, with a strange, shuffled walk that showed little confidence, and glasses that looked better suited to Jeffrey Dahmer.

"Hi," he said timidly, and she couldn't tell if it was an act. He lifted a hand and waved at her.

"Charlie?"

"Yes. Gosh, you are… I mean, you're even more beautiful than your photo…"

"Thanks."

"I'm sorry. I don't mean to be forward. I'm awfully nervous…"

There was a moment of silence.

"So are you ready?"

"Ready?"

"Yes. The hotel room."

He looked around. It was a lovely day, the sun was shining, and people were walking their dogs through the park where they'd arranged to meet.

"Don't you want to go for a walk first?"

She stepped forward. Grinned. Rested her hand lightly on his crotch, and said slowly and deliberately, "No."

He nodded, and she wondered how many times he'd done this before.

He rushed to the car and she followed with a devious stride. He climbed in, and she followed. The car seats were red. A quiet static noise came from the radio. The ignition churned as he turned the key. He checked his mirrors, checked them again, and pulled away.

"So do you do this often?" she asked, watching the world pass through her window. She recognised a café she used to go to with Mum when she was little. They hadn't been there in years. It looked like it was closing down.

"What do you mean?"

"Meeting up with girls." She turned and surveyed the awkwardly unattractive dork beside her. His top button was done up and it made him look strangely formal. "I bet they are lining up down the street for you."

He blushed. "No. You're my first."

"Am I actually, Charles? Because I've been burned before."

He smiled. "Fine. There was one other. But she didn't stick around."

"What happened?"

"She ran as soon as she saw me. Said I was too old. Too weird-looking That's why I was honest with you about how old I am—I don't want to start this relationship on a lie."

"Relationship?"

"Yes, I, I mean, if that's what you want."

"Why don't we stick with this afternoon, Charles?"

"Yes, quite, I—I didn't mean to be keen, I mean—I haven't freaked you out, have I?" She didn't answer and he repeated the question with more urgency, "Have I?"

"No, Charles," she said slowly, enunciating his name in the seductive way she'd seen Marilyn Monroe do in the movies. "You have not."

They reached a set of traffic lights on red and he brought the car to a halt. A broken stop sign lay on the pavement. A street to her left was blocked off with cones and a sign saying *no entry.* On her right was a row of derelict houses with boarded-up windows and overgrown lawns.

He looked at her and tried to smile, though his eyes remained wide, and it looked a little freaky. His eyes wandered downwards and settled on her legs—she'd worn a short, summery white dress with red flowers on—then he took them away abruptly, as if realising he'd been staring. He shifted in his seat and readjusted his jeans around his crotch. She stifled a laugh at his obvious erection.

"Are you okay?" she asked.

She dropped her head to the side and allowed one of her pigtails to flop over her face.

"Yes."

The light turned green.

He drove in silence.

She placed a hand on his thigh. "Are you sure?"

He gulped and nodded.

She removed her hand and turned to the window, covering her mouth, trying not to giggle at this man.

Was this who she was supposed to fear? The predator they'd warned her about? The scary groomer on the internet?

This man was a joke.

He wasn't scary. He wasn't menacing. He wasn't even strong—his arms were bony, and he slouched forward, and she imagined that she probably packed a bigger punch than he did.

What was it everyone was so scared of?

This surely was not it.

He turned into the hotel car park and parked in a space under the shadow of the building. He turned the engine off and stared at the gearbox, a perfect spot between the two of them, and she waited for him to move.

"Are you okay?" she asked.

"Yep."

"Are you going to book a room?"

He took a quick intake of breath and rushed out of the car. She watched him shuffle to the reception and push the glass door open with his shoulder. His limbs were chaotic and seemed to move out of sync; there was no coherence to his walk. She wondered if he still lived with his mother. Perhaps he took residence in her basement. She wondered what he did for a living, imagining him as a dishwasher that no one spoke to, or a creepy cleaner who mumbled to themselves, or a weird school caretaker that all the kids stayed away from.

She checked her reflection. Her lipstick was pink and

childish, her pigtails like her mother used to do them in junior school, and her dress was low enough to show what little cleavage she could boast with such small breasts.

He knocked on the window and it made her jump.

He held up some keys. She stepped out of the car, taking as much time as she wanted, and collected her satchel. She elevated herself onto her tiptoes until her face was an inch from his, took the keys, winked at him, and walked on. She heard him lock his car, followed by the shuffling of his feet behind her.

The room was number forty-two, which was up some steps and on the second floor. She led the way, with him following behind her like a naughty child on the way to the principal's office.

She walked into the room. He followed. She locked the door and sauntered in, eyeing the amenities—of which there were few.

He remained by the door.

She opened the bathroom and looked around. The corners of the mirror had peeled, there was mould on the wall over the shower, and the showerhead kept dripping. Back inside the bedroom, the duvet had a tacky floral pattern just like the last one, and the thick, sickly brown curtains blocked out the light.

"Are you coming in?" she asked, placing her satchel on the floor beside the bed.

He hobbled in, holding his arms across his body like he was cold, and staring at her like she was the one who was meant to initiate things.

She waited for him to do what he needed to do… but he didn't. There was no camera this time, no forcing her onto the bed, no broken promises.

It was up to her this time.

She walked up to him. Stopped. Licked her lips and undid the first button on his shirt. Then the next. Then the next.

He was shaking.

"Are you okay?" she asked.

"Just nervous."

"Me too."

"Really?"

"Yes."

"Can I… touch you?"

She took his hands and placed them on her hips.

He leant his face toward hers. His breath smelt like garlic and cheese. His lips were dry and cracked. They met hers and his tongue entered her mouth and it was slimy and he kept flicking it and too much of his saliva entered her mouth and it almost made her choke. But she let him kiss her. She let him because it meant his eyes were closed, and she could reach into her pocket, and take hold of the sedative, and take it out, and get ready to–

He turned her around and shoved her onto the bed with such surprise and such force that she dropped the sedative and collapsed; her face pushed hard into the duvet, choking on the stench of damp. She reached for the syringe, but he was on top of her and pressing her into the duvet before she could stop it from rolling under the bed.

"Shit…"

He grabbed her hair and dragged her across the bed and lifted her dress and pulled down her underwear and unbuckled his belt and she struggled—went to turn around—but his sudden force and sudden strength was too unexpected and he easily shoved her back down and held her in the position he wanted her in, flat out on the bed, face into the greasy bedsheets, and she could do nothing but play dead and let him do what he had to do.

He was bigger than Adam had been. It hurt more. It was even more forceful, aggressive; he kept pulling himself out and shoving himself back in as far as he could reach, and she could feel it deep inside her, thick and bulging, dry like sand-paper against her insides.

He lowered his face to her ear and said, "I am going to wreck you." His voice sounded mad. Like a deranged clown, or a psychotic monster. The mask of introversion he'd worn, the one of social awkwardness, the façade that would make even the most cynical of women say, "Oh, no, Charles isn't capable of that"—it was gone, and the bull was unleashed. He was the lion who'd made everyone believe it ate leaves; the gecko who'd used camouflage to trick its prey; the serpent who'd tricked the purest of women into picking the deadliest of apples. The velvet glove was so soft that no one knew there was a fist beneath it; he'd perfected the image of someone too weak and uninteresting to pose a threat—but if there's anything the Rolfs and the Epsteins and the Savilles of the world have taught is, it's that the best act like the best to make us unable to conceive of their worst.

He was heavy. His breath on her ear was hot. And every movement inside of her was another jolt of red-hot agony. This was not for her pleasure; it probably wasn't even for his —this was purely for her pain.

Yet, as she squirmed over the bedsheets, his heaving body prompting an unintentional cry upon each thrust, she could see the tip of the syringe beneath the bed.

She draped her arm over the side of the bed, casually, like her body was flopping in subservience, as if she was playing dead to appease him, ensuring he didn't find the movement suspicious, and she stretched her fingers out and reached for it.

Her finger tips scraped the edge, but it was too far away.

He pulled out of her and, for a brief few seconds, she thought it was over—then he shoved himself into her arsehole with so much force that, when he pulled out, she felt shit dribble down her labia.

It didn't bother him. He went in again just as hard, and

pulled out with just as much ferocity, forcing another warm gunk of diarrhoea to slither down her dry cunt.

This was what he was truly capable of. This weak-willed, shy man who could barely look Briony in the eye—*this* was who he really was. And it wasn't that his persona was necessarily fake, just well-constructed. A lie that's believed becomes the truth, and it is only behind a locked door where that truth changes.

And this man had changed.

But he'd been careful. You can read the messages yourself —she was the one who'd suggested meeting. She was at the age of consent. The CCTV showed her getting out of his car and leading him into the hotel, and the footage in the corridor showed her entering the room first.

Every piece of evidence showed her instigating this, so honestly, who was going to believe her when she cried *rape*?

He was a physically weak, socially awkward recluse who held the door open for his colleagues and visited his grandma. Not a predator. Someone strange and uncouth, sure, but he wasn't capable of this—not with this amount of planning and foresight. He was just lonely, and she knew this, the silly girl —why prey on the kindness of an outcast who was obviously so vulnerable?

In fact, the amount of time I've spent trying to convince you of how and why he changed so quickly from this weak, pathetic man to this devious, overpowering sex pest is, in itself, evidence of how easily he could convince people of his truth. People might claim he's the real victim—that is how fucked up this is!

But she had plans.

Oh, how she had plans.

All she needed was the syringe, and she stretched her arm, hoping to reach it.

He was too busy shoving himself harder inside of her to notice, using her defecation as lubricant to help him slop in and out, the squelching noise growing louder and quicker; it hurt so much that it sent fire up her colon.

Her fingertips scraped the end of the syringe, but she merely nudged it further under the bed.

He penetrated harder, further inside, like he was trying to hit her bowels, and he held it inside of her as his erection pulsated and pushed against her intestinal wall. He was grunting now. Harder. Louder. Wailing like the screech of a dying animal, his body spasming with the throbs of ejaculation.

Her rectal tissue bled and dripped onto the sheets.

She nudged the syringe toward the edge of the shadow of the bed, and it took a few attempts, but it eventually moved to within her reach.

She wept. She didn't mean to, it just hurt too much. She bawled as she bled and shat and bled and shat and, with a renewed determination to stop this bastard, she threw her arm under the bed and wrapped her fist around the syringe.

She looked over her shoulder and glimpsed his contorting, twisting face as he reached the peak of his climax.

She shoved the needle into his leg and pushed down on the plunger.

He yelped and fell on top of her. He was unconscious within seconds.

His body was heavy, and she struggled to push him off; he was still inside of her, his body weight pressing down on her back, still firing the last few squirts of jizz up her anal canal.

With a huge heave, she pushed him a little further off her, but she couldn't release herself from his cock, which remained lodged inside of her via a thick mess of bloody shitty spunk.

She reached her arms behind herself and, with all the force her muscles could manage, pushed against his hips. She freed herself from him with a burst of trembling fire. She felt relief, followed by stinging that travelled from her crotch to her bowels, followed by the sensation that something was still inside of her, pushing at the inner walls of her rectum.

She pushed him up and, with another big heave, shoved him hard enough to the side to allow herself to slide out from beneath him. She rolled off the bed and collapsed on the floor, where she remained, huffing, trying to catch her breath. She tried sitting up, but she couldn't bear the pain the movement caused in her insides. Instead, she used the side of the bed to drag herself to her knees whilst keeping her back straight.

She looked down at her legs. A puddle of shitbloodcum had already accumulated on the carpet.

It was at this point that Briony left.

Her body remained, but she stepped aside, and the beautiful Rage stood forward.

Rage had more strength than Briony, and could endure the anguish, and could turn him over with far more ease.

His eyes remained closed, but his scrawny, pimpled body was exposed, lying on a pile of their combined fluids. His mouth was open like he was shocked, his wonky teeth outlining his mangy tongue. She placed a foot on the other side of his head, squatted, and waited for all the shitbloodcum to fall out of her, slopping onto his lips and down his throat.

As Rage did this, she wondered where to start.

Her satchel remained next to the bed. It had everything she needed. She would start with the restraints, hogtying him before fixing his bound wrists and ankles to the bedposts. Then she would open the satchel and he would see just what Rage was capable of.

She was fury, she was lust, she was innocence; she was everything you hate to desire in one virtuous ball of fire.

She was a freak occurrence, like cold rain in a scorching summer.

She was a curse. A disease. A rabid animal.

She was the beautiful combination of all that men truly dreaded. The Castratice inside every villainess.

She was excited. She was ready. She was justified.

And no one would ignore her when they learned about what she did in self-defence this time.

But first, Rage would have a shower. She wanted to be presentable for when it started.

SATCHEL CONTENTS CHECKLIST

- Shower gel
- Shampoo
- Mobile phone (turned off)
- Restraints
- Rope
- Ball gag
- Clamp
- Biology textbook
- Fish hook
- Collapsible metal rod
- Lubricant
- Knife

CHAPTER SEVENTEEN

She sat in the wicker chair in the corner of the room against a faded cushion. Her body was fresh and clean from the shower, and she felt energised and ready.

But she was also patient.

She would do nothing until he woke up.

Rage wanted him to experience everything.

Outside was dark by the time his eyes opened. She knew Mum would be panicking by now, trying desperately to find her, probably even calling the police, her fear intensified by experience. If she'd left her phone on, she'd probably have had a lot of missed calls.

But she'd turned it off.

Rage did not wish to be disturbed.

His eyelids flickered, his eyes opened, and she enjoyed watching his pupils dilate and widen as realisation overcame him; the slow readjustment, the sight of her waiting, the sinister intensity of her smile, the moment he tried to move then found he couldn't, when he realised his hands and feet were hogtied together behind his back and he was as helpless as a pig in a butcher.

"Hi," she said, and he cried out.

She was hoping they could talk first, that she could tease him a little, but it didn't seem plausible—the noise was too great and she didn't want to be disturbed by someone complaining. So she retrieved the ball gag from her satchel and shoved it in his gob. He resisted, and she slapped him, hard, and he wept, and *shitting hell* if that was enough to make him weep then he was *fucked* for what was to come.

She strapped the ball gag around the back of his head and he tried to scream, but it was muffled. She laughed at him, openly, loud and mockingly, deliberate, ensuring that he felt humiliated.

Men can't handle humiliation—any woman who's been met with an aggressive reaction for rejecting a man's advances will tell you that. Humiliation creates a feeling of emasculation, and men are conditioned into believing there is nothing worse than being emasculated. Therefore, she was going to emasculate him as much as her small, delicate hands would allow.

She bent over him until her face was inches from his, and she whispered in his ear, breathing her hot breath against his skin, so close it made his ear wet: "I am going to *wreck* you."

He tried to speak, tried to beg, tried to plead, but it all came out as noise, and he sounded like an imbecile, and it was pathetic, and the emasculation just got worse and worse.

She walked behind him. He tried to rotate himself around to watch her, but he couldn't; his hogtied hands held him in place.

He wasn't moving anywhere.

Which meant he couldn't see what Rage was doing, he just had to guess, had to imagine it, had to feel it—which was going to make it oh, so much worse.

She took some lubricant out of her satchel and held it in front of his face.

"I was going to use this," she said. "You know, to make it

easier." She whispered in his ear again. "But seeing as you didn't give me such a courtesy…"

He screamed another muffled scream, and she grinned a wide, malicious grin as she threw the lubricant into the small tin bin.

She removed the clamp from the bag. She used to watch her dad do woodwork as a child—he made the dining table and chairs they have dinner on, as well as a few bookcases—and she would watch as he used this clamp to fix things to his workbench. That had been years ago, and he had done little woodwork since, and the clamp had grown old and rusty, and its metal points had grown oh so much sharper.

She wound the clamp so that its jaws were together and held it in her mouth as she crawled onto the bed. She put her left hand on his left buttock, her right hand on the other, and stretched his arsehole as wide as it could go. It was hairy and sticky and gross and, if it weren't for the eager anticipation of what she was about to do, it may have revolted her. As it was, once she had stretched it as wide as she could force it to go (which wasn't that wide), she held the buttocks apart with one hand, collected the clamp from between her teeth with her spare hand, and placed the two jaws inside his anus.

Oh, how he wished to cry out—oh, how he wished to scream—oh, how he wished to object—but he could only whimper through the ball that choked him; although a lone tear did drop from his eye and land on the bedsheet.

Rage cackled at the sight.

She shoved the jaws further in, punching the end of the clamp to ensure it was lodged as far into his rectum as it would go, making sure it was lodged inside and wasn't coming out. And, to make doubly sure, she retrieved duct tape from her satchel, stuck it across the end of the clamp, then wrapped it around the front of his crotch (squashing his cock against his body as she did) and wrapped it back around the clamp to ensure it was fixed securely in place.

Then she turned the handle, which stretched the jaws further apart.

His moans intensified. His body was shaking. His cheeks were red. He was trying to beg then trying to scream then trying to beg then trying to scream, but all Rage heard were the pathetic whimpers of a man who was as pitiable as he was tragic.

She turned the handle again, and the jaws moved, and his anus widened further.

He cried. The screams and begs had stopped, and he was crying furious tears. They crashed on the bedsheets and flooded down his cheeks.

She turned the handle again and opened the jaws to about an inch. In each movement, another burst of pain came out of his mouth, only to be muzzled by his gag. His fists were clenching. His feet were twirling. But it was the only movement he could make, aside from the trembling of his entire body.

She turned the handle again and stretched it another inch.

He cried harder, then harder still.

Shook harder.

Wept harder.

She turned the handle again, then again, then again, another inch with each rotation, until his anus began resisting, until she had reached the limit of how far it would stretch—then she turned the handle again, gripping it with both hands, putting all her dainty muscle behind it, and forced it another inch.

His anal tissue bled. The sensitive skin ripped. It dribbled at first, sliding down his thigh, then bled harder, different patches of his sphincter opening up into dots of red.

She gave it one last rotation, and it really resisted, so she had to try really hard, until she was wet with sweat, and with every weep he gave, she knew she was succeeding.

When she'd stretched it as far as it could go, she stepped back and admired her work.

Blood gushed down his thighs, over the duct tape, over the bedsheets, mixing with the stains of the shitbloodcum that had fallen out of her. His body rattled, his tears fell, his screams entwined with begs entwined with weeps and she imagined how much it must hurt—but she didn't need to imagine. He may not have stretched her this much, but he had stretched her pretty far.

She sighed, opened her satchel, and took out a textbook. She had borrowed it from her biology class—her teacher would never notice—and she opened it to the page that provided a diagram of the interior anatomy of a human. She placed it on the bed beside his leg.

Her teacher had told her class that the large intestine was about five feet long, and Rage wondered how much of it she could pull out.

She stuck her hand into her satchel of treasures once again and pulled out a small fishhook. She pressed the end against her finger and pricked a dab of blood. She took out a small metal rod—one that she could stretch to three times its size. It was supposed to reach about a metre in length. That would do. She attached the fishhook to the end of the rod, and it dangled there like a bit of loose skin.

She took a big, deep breath, and said to herself, "Here goes." She was nervous. She had done nothing like this before, and we all get slightly anxious when it's our first time.

She held the rod above her head with both hands, placed the tip of the hook into his anus, and slowly lowered the rod inside. After an inch or two of insertion, it met a brief resis-tance; it became caught on an open wound around his rectal tissue, but with a bit of force she shoved it in. It tore up the tissue and more blood came gushing out, but it was fine—she was hardly expecting the fish hook to be clean when she was done, was she?

After the tip of the rod had made its way inside, she inserted the rest like she was taking a shot with a snooker cue, resting her left hand at the base of his ball sack and pushing the rod further in with her right hand. He screamed and kept crying and shaking and all that—by now, that's a given—but she didn't pay attention to it. This was tricky, and she needed to concentrate on what she was doing.

Once the rod was about a foot in, she returned to the diagram in the textbook and used it as a guide. The intestine was further up, so she pushed the end of the rod downwards, hoping the fish hook would go higher. It became caught on something again, but a big shove forced it further in.

She kept going and going, another foot in, then another, but struggled at the end when she only had the last few inches of the rod to go—the rod would not go further in. She could wiggle it a little, but when she pushed it there felt like there was something spongy at the other end, and it had reached its limit.

She paused to see how he was doing. She gave him a playful smack on the bum cheek and walked around to his face. She crouched in front of him and gave him a big smile.

"How's it going?" she asked. "I realise I haven't been paying much attention to you—I'm afraid I've been concentrating. What are..."

She grew distracted by something, and she had to turn away from his sweaty, twisting, contorting face—there was a problem at the other end.

The blood.

There was just too much of it.

It was gushing and gushing past the end of the rod.

She quickly took hold of it, her hands becoming coated in thick dark red liquid, and tried to pull it out. Her hands were too sticky and just kept sliding off the rod, so she had to shove a few of her fingers into his anus to get more leverage—which was easy to do, as the clamp was quite wide and there were still a few centimetres around the rod.

With a big heave, she pulled on the rod, and he squealed against the ball gag, and she pulled again and the entire rod came out along with a large, semi-flat tube attached to the fishhook. She stepped back, bringing the rod with her, and much of his intestine came out with it, as well as something else that was slightly oval shaped (the liver maybe?)

It was at this point she dropped the rod, picked up a towel to wipe the blood off her hands (although it was all over her clothes as well—she considered another shower, but it would probably look better if she was covered in violence when the police got here), and surveyed her work.

He had stopped squealing and crying. Unfortunately, he was dead. Which was a shame, as she had more things planned.

She sighed.

Ah well.

She removed the hogties and placed them around her wrists and ankles, hard, to ensure that the indents of them were on her skin as well. She shoved him off the bed, then laid in the shitbloodcum, rolling around until her entire body was covered in the chaos.

She took her phone from the satchel and switched it on. Sure enough, there were 42 missed calls from her mother.

She went to call 999, then remembered—the clamp was still on him! Whoopsy.

She took the clamp off, put it in the satchel, and took out her knife. She needed to make it look like a frenzied attack in self-defence, so she stabbed him, over and over, all across his chest and his neck, blood squirting like a jet from a water fountain on each strike.

Then she paused.

Looked around the room.

It was carnage. It was havoc. It was mayhem.

But to Rage, it was justice. It was acceptance. It was beauty.

She stood. Bounced from foot to foot. Made herself out of breath, dialled 999, then ran out of the room screaming, shoving herself from wall to wall of the corridor, begging people for help.

The operator answered, and she gave her truth of what had happened.

999 CALL TRANSCRIPT

Call Handler
Hello, which service do you require?

Briony
Police!

Call Handler
Police emergency, can I take your name?

Briony
Hello (…) please help it (…) it's (…) it's Bri (…) Briony.

Call Handler
How can I help you?

Briony
I was attacked (…) this man (…) he met me online (…) he attack (…) attacked me.

Call Handler
Okay Briony stay calm (…) where is this man now?

Briony

In bed (…) in the hotel room.

Call Handler

Is he in the room with you now?

Briony

No I (…) I'm out.

Call Handler

Are you able to leave the hotel safely?

Briony

He (…) he's dead.

Call Handler

He's dead?

Briony

Yes.

Call Handler

How did he die Briony?

Briony

I (…) I had to do it (…) he attacked (…) he attacked me.

Call Handler

I understand (…) can you confirm your location for me?

Briony

I'm in a hotel (…) the Jayside or Jacksonside or Jolside or something or (…) please help (…) please come quick (…) I'm scared.

Call Handler

I have your location Briony (…) police are on their way now (…) they won't be long.

Briony

Thank you (…) thank you so much (…) he hurt me (…) he hurt me so bad.

Call Handler

I know Briony (…) it's okay (…) they won't be long.

Briony

Thank you (…) thank you.

CHAPTER EIGHTEEN

A group of police officers entered the hotel, including DCI Kevin McCluskey, and Briony flung herself upon him like a child upon a parent.

She'd been building herself up for this, bouncing from foot to foot, tearing up her eyes, pinching her skin to illicit pain, convincing herself of the lie so her truth would be more convincing: She was the victim. She was the one who was hurt. She was the one who was tricked.

She was the weak little girl, and he was the big scary man.

And oh, how persuasive she was! Her distraught demeanour eradicated any element of doubt in her saviour, forcing her truth to become his truth. Her performance was worthy of any acting award.

And she knew how to play this man.

The White Knight Syndrome was never more present than in a policeman, and she preyed on it with such ease that she almost broke character to laugh at him. Her puppy dog eyes brought out his paternal instincts, and when he looked at her, he could only see a fragile creature in need of protection—a perfect disguise for the powerful beast within.

Oh, how a late-middle-aged man raised in patriarchy loves

nothing more than the opportunity to rescue a weak little girl in a heroic act of chivalry.

He told her it was okay, but she was too inconsolable, too unable to control her emotions. She was HYSTERICAL—an outdated adjective to describe women who are considered irrational and easily unhinged by the slightest increase of emotion, as if a small sign of violence would be enough to make her swoon—but she played the part expertly—and by wailing and sobbing and squealing and wobbling and weeping and diving into his arms and pressing her wet cheeks against his chest and pleading for the big strong man to take her away, she became absolutely, unequivocally, unobtrusively, indisputably hysterical.

She was carried away by the big hero, taken down the steps, thrashing her arms and kicking her legs until, finally, she calmed down and wrapped her arms around the man carrying her out. She cried into his lapels until they were drenched with tears. She held him close to make him think he was needed; to make him feel an emotional connection that would stop him from seeing the crime scene as it was.

He placed her in the back of a police car and fetched her a bottle of water.

Water.

That's what he gave a victim—water.

As far as he was concerned, she'd just come out of a big, bad, bloody battle with a man much older than her—*again*—and he brought her a bottle of H2O.

These guys had no clue how to deal with a victim.

He sat with her and told her to breathe. As if being attacked means you forget how to breathe—she was panting like hell for Christ's sake—yet he put his palms face down, exhaled slowly, and mansplained how to breathe.

She wanted to spit in his face.

But she didn't. She calmed her breathing, but kept the tears going, snorting, and he gave her a tissue, and she blew her nose, and he asked her if she needed anything.

Yeah, a police officer with a fucking brain.

"No... No, I'm okay..."

She wiped her eyes. Wiped her nose. Looked down.

"I'm going to have one of my officers take you back to the station," he told her, his voice so calm she couldn't ever imagine it angry. "Then we'll talk more there."

She nodded. Sniffed.

He stood. Waved someone over. An overzealous woman who looked too young to work in the police hurried over, dressed in bright clothing, and Briony hated her the instant she saw her.

"Hey, friend!" the woman said, and why was she so happy, Briony had just been viciously assaulted. "How are you?"

Fucking brilliant you stupid bint.

"I dunno..."

"My name is Sunny!" Of course it was. "I'm a victim support officer. I'm here to make sure you are taken care of during the whole day's events, okay?"

Hasn't a victim been through enough pain?

"Okay..."

"I'm not going to ask you how you're feeling, because that would be a silly question right now, wouldn't it?"

Was she... was she supposed to respond?

"But I am going to sit next to you while we go to the police station, if that's okay? At least until your mother arrives. I won't leave your side."

I'd rather gouge my eyes out with a kitchen fork.

"You promise?"

She smiled, and Briony had never realised someone could smile in such an annoying way. "I promise."

She asked Briony to budge over—because for some reason she couldn't just walk around to the other side of the car to get in

—and she sat next to Briony for what was going to be the most excruciating car ride of her life. She fully expected this woman to be talking about rainbows and singing kumbaya by the end of it.

As they took off, and Sunny's incessant voice kept talking, Briony managed to tune it out. She gave an occasional grunt of acknowledgement to keep Sunny satisfied, but Briony's focus was on watching the hotel grow smaller in the distance.

Kevin watched them go, then dressed himself in personal protective clothing and entered the crime scene. He thought it would be a fairly standard crime scene—a body, some bodily fluids, evidence of a struggle—but he could never have anticipated what he was about to find.

CHAPTER NINETEEN

DCI Kevin McCluskey was a hardened police officer who'd been to many murder scenes, and seen many bodies, and witnessed many savage acts of violence, and experienced the aftermath of the worst parts of human nature—but even he struggled to suppress the need to gag.

Feral beasts destroyed their prey with more conservatism than this girl had.

If he had not known who had caused this despicable scene, he might have guessed that it was an escaped lion, or a notorious psychopath, or a crazed animal—but even then, he wouldn't have anticipated staring at the innards that had been forcibly removed from a human being. The bed looked like a butcher's bin; a monsoon of thick, red blood; a Picasso if he'd used human remains instead of paint. The wall was more blood than it was wall, and the carpet was stained with such intense dark red that it was hard to know what colour it used to be. It was almost impossible to describe the room without overusing the word *blood*—bloody walls, bloody body, bloody floor, bloody ceiling, bloody bed, bloody chair, bloody door...

An ocean of blood with lumps of this guy's insides like the texture of Grandma's Chicken Noodle Soup.

It was hard to say if the violence she had committed had been premeditated, as he couldn't imagine such destruction ever being planned. It was haphazard and reckless, a disgusting meld of opportunity and impulsivity.

But there was a satchel. Open. Containing instruments that could only have one purpose.

Was this *his* satchel?

Surely, it was...

What was the alternative—that she'd lured him here with a bag of items and grave, devious intentions?

Would a vulnerable young girl such as this be capable of tricking an experienced predator who knew how to get away with his repugnant acts?

Kevin put his hands on his hips. He was hesitant to entertain such thoughts. He'd worked hard during his time as detective chief inspector to change attitudes toward female victims—to end the gaslighting, the victim-blaming, the disbelief. There were still a lot of misinformed officers, but he'd made progress with many of his staff. He was therefore, understandably, hesitant to imagine that this girl could have acted in anything more than self-defence.

But this guy wasn't killed in self-defence. He was butchered in a prolonged act of torture.

Could it be trauma? One can't underestimate the devastating effect of this girl's first assault, and it could have meant that a second assault resulted in a more extreme, violent self-defence response; an unleashing of a survivor's fury. She could have reacted in a way that was reasonable to what she'd been through.

Even so, something felt wrong.

Once the scene of crime officers had extracted their samples and taken their photos, they began bagging and removing the evidential items. When he noticed the satchel being removed, he asked his officer to stop. He wasn't sure why. It was instinct. Years and years of experience had given him this instinct, and he'd learned to trust it.

"Was this his bag?" Kevin asked, expecting to receive a shrug, as if this officer would have any idea.

But his officer didn't shrug. Instead, the officer held the bagged item between them and showed Kevin the label that had been sewn onto the inside of the satchel.

Property of Briony Spector.

Kevin bowed his head and rubbed his sinus.

"Thank you," he grunted, and encouraged the officer to move along.

He remained stationary as officers moved past him, a hectic scene of officers collecting evidence while he remained motionless, lost in thought. No matter how much he ruminated over it, he wasn't sure what to think.

He needed to interview the girl.

He returned to his car and made his way back to the station.

POLICE INTERVIEW TRANSCRIPT

Kevin

The time is 11:32 p.m. and we have begun recording (…) present are DCI Kevin McCluskey (…) Briony Spector (…) and Mrs Beatrice Spector (…) Briony's mother and appropriate adult (…) Briony (…) just to make you aware (…) you are not under arrest (…) but I am still going to remind you that you do not have to say anything but it may harm your defence if you do not mention when questioned something you may later rely on in court (…) anything you do say may be given in evidence (…) okay?

Beatrice

If she's not under arrest then why are you cautioning her?

Kevin

We just wish to make her aware of her rights.

Beatrice

But why (…) she was attacked.

Kevin

That is what we are going to establish.

Beatrice

What do you mean establish (…) Kevin? (…) if she hasn't–

Briony

Mum it's fine (…) just (…) get on with it.

Kevin

So Briony (…) in your own words (…) and in your own time (…) explain to me what happened.

Briony

Okay (…) well (…) I, er (…) I met Charles online (…) in a chatroom where he (…) he seemed really nice (…) I knew after (…) after what happened before that (…) that I had to be careful (…) and I was (…) but I was on my own all the time because Mum was busy with Shane and my friends were (…) were (…) not like (…) being like they were (…) so I spoke to him and he seemed really nice and he seemed kind and so I said we should meet and he said yes (…) and then we met and went to this hotel (…) it was (…) wasn't very nice.

Kevin

What wasn't very nice?

Briony

Well he was all friendly and a little chatty and quite timid and I (…) I liked that about him (…) but er (…) then he…

Kevin

Then he what Briony?

Briony

[Remains silent]

Kevin

That's okay (...) tell me in your own time.

Briony

[Remains silent]

Kevin

How old did he tell you he was?

Briony

I don't know (...) older.

Kevin

So he didn't give you his age?

Briony

Yes (...) he did (...) forty-two I think.

Kevin

Did that concern you?

Briony

No (...) yes (...) I guess (...) I dunno (...) he seemed nice (...) not like the other (...) the last (...) the guy before (...) he seemed friendly (...) I trusted him.

Kevin

Can you tell me anymore about what happened in the hotel room?

Briony

Yes (...) I (...) sorry it's not (...) it's...

Kevin

I understand (...) take your time.

Briony

Well (…) we were in the room and then (…) then he (…) he started being forceful with me and he pushed me down and got on top of me and he (…) he put (…) he put it inside of me (…) and then he (…) he put it inside…

Kevin

Go on Briony (…) you're doing really well.

Briony

He put it (…) put it inside my bum.

Beatrice

[Gasps]

Briony

And I told him to stop and he didn't and he got more forceful and it made me (…) poo (…) and I was bleeding and he kept going and then I noticed he had a (…) a needle in his bag and I thought (…) well (…) is that going to put me to sleep (…) was he going to use it on me (…) was he going to kill me (…) I've seen it on the news when (…) when they do that (…) and so I grabbed it (…) the needle (…) and I jabbed it into him and he (…) he (…) I grabbed it and put it in him and he went asleep and then I (…) I killed him (…) I didn't know what else to do I'm so sorry I just thought if he woke up again then he would hurt me and I didn't know how long he was going to be out for and I didn't want him to hurt me again like the last guy and–
[Sobbing]

Kevin

That's okay Briony (…) take your time.

Briony

Then I rang 999.

Kevin
And what happened then?

Briony
Then the police showed up and that's when you were there.

Kevin
Okay (…) you say you took the needle from the bag (…) did you take anything else from the bag?

Briony
He had a lot of (…) a lot of utensils (…) so I used some (…) to make sure he didn't get up again.

Kevin
Which ones did you use?

Briony
I (…) do I have to talk about this now?

Kevin
No Briony (…) not if you don't feel comfortable (…) but this is your opportunity to give your account.

Briony
He just (…) I was so scared.

Kevin
I understand (…) what can you tell me about this bag?

Briony
He had all this stuff in.

Kevin
And did he bring this bag with him?

Briony
Yes (…) I think so.

Kevin
I have a question for you now Briony (…) and I want you to think carefully how you answer.

Briony
Okay.

Kevin
Inside that bag that you say he brought (…) is a label with a name on (…) what can you tell me about that?

Briony
Label?

Kevin
Yes (…) here have a look (…) for the record I am showing Briony Exhibit 7c (…) a picture of the name label inside the satchel found at the scene (…) whose name is that Briony?

Briony
Mine.

Kevin
And so you're saying this is the bag he brought?

Briony
…No.

Kevin
This is not the bag he brought?

Briony

No (…) it isn't.

Kevin

But you told me it is.

Briony

No (…) he brought another bag (…) this was my bag (…) he put the items from his bag into mine (…) I don't know why (…) I think my bag was bigger maybe.

Kevin

Okay (…) so to clarify (…) he brought the items in a different bag then put them in yours?

Briony

Yes.

Kevin

Do you have any ideas why he may have done this?

Briony

No.

Kevin

Okay (…) is there anything else you can tell us about what happened today?

Briony

No (…) I mean (…) no (…) I just (…) can I go home now (…) I want to go home.

Kevin

Of course (…) I am stopping the recording at 11.50 p.m.

CHAPTER TWENTY

With the care for which one might use when handling a new-born baby, Kevin placed a coffee in front of Beatrice Spector and settled himself in the plastic chair opposite her.

She had been hesitant to leave her daughter alone, but Kevin had insisted that they talk, and she was concerned for what he had to say. She knew Kevin well, and she respected him as both an officer and a person. Even so, Kevin knew she detected something different in the way he was avoiding her eyes. Her coffee remained untouched and she watched him with an intensity that made him uncomfortable. He urged himself to say what he was thinking, but it was hard to verbalise his thoughts when they made such little sense.

"I'm just going to come out with what I have to say," he began. "I'm not even sure what my thoughts are yet, but... there's something wrong."

"What is it?"

"I don't know yet. It's just Briony's story—it doesn't add up."

"What do you mean, it doesn't add up? What are you suggesting?"

He sighed. Leant back. Hesitated. For a seasoned officer who'd dealt with many difficult parents, he was doing an awful job of this. He rubbed the sweat from his brow and leant forward.

"I've spent quite a bit of time at the crime scene. The man she met was ripped apart from the inside. This wasn't a quick murder—this was prolonged."

"You're suggesting my daughter tortured the man?"

"No. Yes. I'm not sure. It just feels wrong."

She looked away in disbelief, her mouth bobbing open.

"Her story about the bag," he said. "She changed it pretty quickly, didn't she?"

"Considering what she has been through—*twice*—I'm not surprised that she is stumbling over her words. Survivors can rarely tell a coherent story at first, surely you know that?"

"Yes, I do. More than anyone."

"Then tell me why you think my daughter did something wrong when she was groomed and assaulted by that man?"

He said nothing. Looked down. Rotated a sachet of sugar that someone had discarded between his thumb and his forefinger. The vending machine in the corner made a strange grinding noise, and the vile obscenities of a rowdy prisoner being coerced by several officers passed the door.

"I don't know," he finally admitted.

He knew why she'd be angry. He too had grown tired of this culture of victim-blaming, and gaslighting, and scepticism toward survivors—and he was hating himself for even doubting anything Briony said. But he was a detective. Scepticism was his job. Interrogating the facts was his job. And, despite the principles he encouraged in his officers, he knew that this girl's reaction to her perpetrator was excessive.

Beyond excessive.

"Is she a murder suspect, Kevin?" she asked.

He didn't answer. Stared at the sugar sachet. Turned it over. And over. And over.

"Kevin?"

He lifted his gaze and met hers. Her eyes were weak and tired; those of a weary mother with an aggressive love for her child. She was the kind of mother he imagined his wife would have been, should their daughter have survived.

"I don't know," he admitted. "Not right now. But there is every chance that the evidence might point us that way."

"The evidence? How exactly does an eighteen-year-old girl, groomed online, *again,* assaulted in a hotel room, *again,* become a murderer when she showed the bravery to defeat her attacker?"

"I can't tell you everything we saw in that hotel room, but if I could—"

"I don't see what you could possibly have found."

"My instinct is—"

"Your instinct? Does that stand up in court?"

He huffed. "My instinct has saved many people."

"And I imagine it's killed many too."

He said nothing. She was angry. He could see that. He would be too. Hell, he was angry with what he was saying, and she wasn't even his child.

"Kevin, you are my friend, and as my friend, I need you to assure me that you are fighting to protect my daughter—not trying to condemn her."

He hesitated. "Of course."

"Good." A long pause. "And is there anything else?"

Yes. There was.

This wasn't the end of the conversation.

The issue wasn't resolved.

But there was nothing else he could say. He'd made his feelings known—poorly—and she had made hers known—excellently—and he could not find the words he needed.

"Just watch her," he said, keeping his voice as soft as he could. "And check there's nothing unusual in her behaviour."

"What would 'unusual behaviour' be for a teenage girl who's survived two assaults?"

"I understand what you're saying—please, just watch her. I'm not comfortable releasing her into your custody unless you agree to be vigilant."

She stood. Shoved the chair under the table, grinding its chair legs across the floor with a loud growl.

"Are we done?"

"Yes."

She went to leave. Paused at the door. Turned back.

"Kevin—please help my daughter."

Kevin nodded. "I will."

She placed her hand on his. Held it for a moment. Then she left.

And he remained sat there. Still. Staring at the space she had just vacated.

He had a lot of work to do. A lot of investigating. A lot of evidence to scrutinise. Tasks to allocate. Witnesses to talk to. A 999 call to listen to.

But he didn't want to.

Because he feared what he might find.

He did not want to arrest a traumatised eighteen-year-old girl for murder.

SCENES OF CRIME REPORT

Supervising Inspector: DCI Kevin McCluskey
Report Completed by: Laurence Wells

INCIDENT REPORT

Case No.
1645968-459-2023

Report Date:
28-04-2023

Report Time:
22:13

Arrival Time:
22:18

Reporting Channel:
The 999 Police Emergency Line

Location of Incident:
Room 42, Jason Hotels, South District Lane,
Gloucester, GL62 0LT

Reporting Officer:
P6596520
D594106

Reporting Witness:
Briony Spector

Reporting Witness ID:
JIFD:H953054(F)

Victim/Reporting Witness Relationship:
Victim met her attacker online.

REPORTING OFFICERS' NARRATIVE:

Responded to 999 call from Briony Spector at Jason Hotels at 22:13 with report that she had been assaulted and killed her attacker in self-defence. Arrived at 22:18 to find Miss Spector in hotel corridor. She was crying, and was difficult to talk to. She was calmed down by DCI Kevin McCluskey and taken to be interviewed with mother present. Inside the hotel room, the corpse was on the floor, on his back. There were multiple stab wounds on his torso and neck. Blood, semen and excrement were on the bedsheets. An empty syringe, an open satchel, a ball gag, rope, metal clamp, rod and fish hook were on the floor. A knife was retrieved from beside the door. What has initially been identified as part of a large intestine was found on the floor also.

Case Classification:

Dead Body Found

Sexual Assault

Rape

Responsible Unit:

Crime Gloucestershire Region

CHAPTER TWENTY-ONE

riony rested her elbow in the open window and her chin on her fist. She watched the world go by as her mother drove, gazing at people they passed: mothers dragging children, women pushing prams, men in suits amid aggressive phone conversations, teenagers showing off, boys on their bikes... It felt strange how everything could change with her, but nothing changed with anyone else.

She grew increasingly aware of her mum's glances. She probably thought they were even discreet—but Briony could feel them, each one brief and intense.

What she couldn't fathom, however, was what they meant.

Mum was almost expressionless, like she was trying to hide her concern, but it kept coming out in twitches of her nose and quivers in her lip. It was the same look she'd had the first time Briony rode a bike, or on Briony's first day at school, or when Briony dove into a swimming pool. Moments she felt terror that her child might not be safe but kept to herself.

"What is it?" Briony snapped. She'd meant to ask it nicely, but it came out with a burst of spite.

"What's what, darling?"

She was calling her *darling*.

She only ever gave Briony pet names when there was something on her mind.

"You keep looking at me," Briony stated.

Mum huffed. Went to speak. Huffed again.

"Why don't you say what you're thinking?" Briony prompted.

"I'm just concerned about you. You've been through a lot. This is too much for a girl your age to handle."

Briony frowned. She wasn't aware that there was an age where her experiences would not be too much.

"I just can't believe this happened to you twice," Mum said, her face twisting as she tried not to cry. "I feel like I'm failing to protect you."

"Great job making it about you, Mum."

"No, that's not what I meant—please don't take it that way. I just feel guilty, and I don't know what to do."

Briony shrugged.

She turned back to the window. Watched a couple on a park bench as they drove past; the way he put his hand on her leg, and the way she smiled like it was a gesture of affection rather a statement of territory. She was probably unaware that he was an arsehole. Then again, he may not be—but the odds weren't in his favour.

"You've been through a lot," Mum said, then covered her face to stifle her tears before returning her hand to the steering wheel. "What you had to do to that man... It was so brave."

"It was me or him, Mum."

"I know. It's just..."

"Just what?"

"It just seems a bit..."

"A bit what?"

"...I don't know."

Briony panicked.

For the first time, she panicked.

Did Mum think she had been excessive? Did the police

think that? Had she hurt the guy too much? Would they be coming for her? Had that police guy already said something?

"It was self-defence, Mum."

"I know, dear, it's just… what did you do in self-defence?"

"You want me to go through it?"

"No. Yes. I mean… I don't know. I just want to understand."

"He was older than me and he tried to fuck me in the arse and so I killed him."

Mum flinched at the word *arse* and the word *fuck,* and Briony hated how the word *fuck* drew a more disgusted response from her than the word *killed.*

Mum went to speak, didn't, tried again, didn't, then blurted out, "But how exactly did you kill him?"

"What?" Briony put on a show of being enraged, curling her fists and strengthening her voice. "Do you want me to go through all the gory details with you? What is wrong with you?"

"I know, I'm sorry, I shouldn't have…"

Mum immediately turned into a layby and brought the car to a stop. She undid her seatbelt so she could get closer to her daughter and threw her arms around her and held her like she might never hold her again.

Briony relished it.

The closeness. The smell of her cheap perfume. The feel of her cosy jacket against her cheek. The dampness of Mum's tears in her hair.

Briony even let herself cry.

She wasn't sure what the tears were for—whether it was the performance, whether she was heavily in role, whether it was the violence of what she'd done, whether it was the anxiety of thinking she'd been suspected; or whether it was simply the feeling of being close to Mum in a way she had craved.

She only seemed to get hugs when she killed perverts.

And this was why she did it. Why she'd torn that man apart. Why she'd let him penetrate her insides so she could impale his.

It was so she could feel like she had a mother.

So she could get the attention her brother received for his anger. So she could have her mother's arms wrapped around her like this. So she could hug back just as tightly, and hold onto her mother so she would not go.

So she would never go.

And they cried together.

And everything came out.

Cars sped by, a bloke stopped and changed a flat tyre, a lorry driver pulled up behind them and pissed in the bushes, black clouds drifted overhead and it rained and then stopped raining—the entire world kept on turning, but she was away from it, here, in the car, in her mother's arms.

Her mother finally went to release her, but Briony didn't let her. She kept her arms around her mother's torso, wanting more, *needing* more.

She let her mother go after another few more minutes.

Mum looked at her, her cheeks red, her eyes damp, her face mirroring her daughters, and there was such adoration and love in those eyes that Briony swore she would keep killing whoever she needed to kill if this was what she earned.

"I love you," Mum said.

"I love you too."

A wet kiss on the forehead and Mum turned back to the steering wheel, pulled onto the road, and drove off.

But when she wasn't changing gears, her hand rested on her daughter's leg.

And Briony's hand rested on Mum's hand.

And she forgot all about the police officer.

But the police officer did not forget about her.

EXTRACT FROM BLOG 'GLOUCESTERSHIRE AND THE GLOBE'

MISFORTUNE STRIKES TWICE WITH FEMALE VICTIM

The teenage girl, now identified as eighteen-year-old Briony Spector from South Gloucester, has been attacked for a second time, months after her first.

The girl was assaulted by a man who groomed her online in early January before killing the perpetrator in self-defence. Yet she allowed herself to be groomed once again, by yet another older man, and this time reacted with even more violence.

Police are yet to confirm whether this apparent act of self-defence is suspicious, but one wonders how a girl suffering from trauma can get herself into the exact same position, just months after taking her rapist's life.

Sources that I cannot name have confirmed that the girl's actions were far more violent this time. There is a suggestion that parts of the man's insides were removed, which begs one question—at what point does self-defence become murder?

Whether this is a vigilante crusade, an act of defiance, or a disturbed little girl, we are yet to know. Some may say they don't care—if someone is killing off the kind of men who would lure a teenage girl to a hotel room, then she's doing the world a service.

But this wasn't just killing. This was torture.

And one must wonder – at what point does the innocent man need to worry?

I will update you as soon as I know more—but I would suggest, in the meantime, if you know this girl, keep your distance.

At least, if you want to keep your spleen.

CHAPTER TWENTY-TWO

B riony did not wait three weeks to return to school this time.

Not that there wasn't the choice—Briony's mother insisted and insisted that Briony could stay at home for as long as she needed. But Briony didn't want to.

She could not wait to return to school.

She recalled how people had treated during her last return to school—the awe, the adoration, the appreciation. Those friends she'd gained who had since grown bored of her would surely be re-energised in their enthusiasm. They had been so amazed by what she did a few months ago that they'd wanted to hear every detail—they'd wanted her to be part of their group, part of their life.

So, after kissing her mum on the cheek, she stepped out of the car, stood with feet shoulder width apart, and grinned at the building that would be the scene of her homecoming.

She imagined the way they would flock toward her when she entered that canteen, how they would wave her over, how they would beckon her to be part of their friendships—how those that Briony did not choose to sit with would glare at those that Briony befriended, distraught that this powerful young girl did not choose to join their table.

She opened the front door, marched in, and nodded at the receptionist.

The receptionist, however, did not nod back.

Instead, she seemed to recoil slightly. Made her body smaller, edged away, looking briefly at Briony then quickly returning her gaze to her screen. There was no hello, no recognition, no welcoming back—just a cold, callous woman who'd rather be rude than say hello to a hero.

Determined not to let this ruin her moment, Briony proceeded through the next set of doors, down the corridor, and toward the canteen, where she was sure everyone would be having breakfast. She could hear the bustling of her peers as she approached, and her smile returned.

She paused outside the doors. Psyched herself up. Jumped up and down a little, feeling a little nervous about all the love she was going to receive, then opened the doors and stepped inside.

A hush descended.

Not a complete silence—but many conversations paused, and everyone's wary eyes turned to her.

There was no beckoning her over, no smiles, no eager requests for her to tell her story. It was a sea of cautious faces.

She shook it off and walked to the set of girls who had previously befriended her. They avoided looking at her.

"Hey guys," she said, forcing them to turn her way.

They said nothing.

"I was wondering if I could sit with you?"

They looked at each other. None of them answered, and none of them moved up to let her on the bench.

"Guys?" she prompted.

Eventually, one of them spoke. "I'm not sure that's a good idea."

"What?"

They looked at each other again. Whispered. Exchanged glances. Then the speaker turned back to her.

"We heard rumours about what you did," she said. "I mean… did you actually do that?"

"Do what?"

Blank faces.

"What do you think I did?" she repeated.

"I heard you tied him up," one replied.

"I heard you tortured him," said another.

"I heard you rolled around his blood and his intestines and that you chopped his cock off," said another.

"I did not chop his cock off!" Briony snapped. Her instincts told her to stop there, but she didn't. "But I would if I had to. I would chop the cock off any guy who tried to rape me. Wouldn't you?"

They exchanged glances again. Briony's fists clenched.

"How do you manage to get raped twice in a matter of months?" the unelected speaker said again.

"He—he—what the hell is wrong with you guys?"

"What's wrong with *us*?"

More glances. Briony felt like gutting all of them.

"We don't think you're safe," said another. "And we want you to stay away from us."

"Stay away from you?" She could feel her eyes welling up. "But—but I thought you guys were my friends…"

"We don't want to be friends with someone who could do the kinds of things you've done."

Briony didn't go anywhere. Not at first. She remained, wanting to argue her case, then wanting to beat the hell out of all of them.

A few of them gripped their cutlery a little tighter. As if preparing for an attack. As if needing to defend themselves.

Before Briony could say anything else, the headmistress appeared at her side.

"Briony?" she said. "What are you doing here?"

"What do you mean, what am I doing here? This is my school!"

The headmistress looked over all the faces in the canteen. They were all staring at Briony. Every single one of them.

"Come with me," the headmistress said, and led Briony out.

Briony followed, her arms wrapped around her body, trying not to look back at all the people gawking at her like she was a zoo exhibit. She could feel Rage pushing at the surface, stretching her skin. She was there, bubbling at the tip of her fingers, twitching her muscles.

The headmistress led Briony to the main school doors, then turned back to her.

"We didn't think you were coming back yet," she told Briony. "And so we haven't put anything in place."

"What do you need to have in place?"

"We need the counsellor to speak to you, we need support in place, a risk assessment—"

"A risk assessment? Why do you need to do a risk assessment on me?"

Rage was ready, begging Briony to let her out, begging to be let free from her cage.

"We need to ensure our students' safety is not put at risk."

"What?"

"Briony, it's best you go home until we have made the appropriate arrangements, okay? I'll call your mother."

Before the headmistress could do such a thing, Briony turned and ran, sprinting away.

Briony was distraught, but Rage had just been fed. And whilst Briony was ready to run home and cry, Rage loved how it tasted.

Little did the headmistress and the students know they had just unleashed the true nature of the beast that dwelled within.

Briony ran home, wiping away tears, desperate for her mother's embrace.

Rage flexed her muscles and stretched her arms.

Both were preparing for what would come next.

ONLINE COMMENT THREAD BELOW NEWS ARTICLE

User61666

Anyone else find it weird that she was groomed twice so quick? Like how does that happen?

User818816

Crackin bit of victim blaming there

User61666

FFS. Just askin the question. Seems a bit stupid to me.

User818816

STUPID? N what bout the guys who groomed her, what names do you have 4 them?

User61666

O fuck off u feminazi bitch. U no wot I was askin.

User818816

Feminazi? LOL. Probly the only 3 syllable word u no. N no, I don't know wot ur saying. There r 2 people to blame 4 this, n neither of them r her.

User61666
Did I say they was? Read wot I wrote u thick cnt. N here is a 3 syllable word 4 u. FUKINSLAG.

User818816
That's 2 words. N yes I read wot u said. U asked how she was so 'stupid' – she is A 18 YR OLD GIRL u misogynistic prick.

User61666
Me misoginystic LOL bet ur a fugly hairy bitch lesbian. Stop bein woke. I was askin a question.

User818816
N ur question was whether a 2 time rape victim was stupid 4 being raped! N no Im not a lesbian, but wiv men like u its real tempting.

User61666
Did I say she was stupid 4 being raped? N if she was askin 4 it then is it rape? she messgd them didnt she? Twice? N she woz 18 – at the age of consent, meanin she woz old enough to fuck wivout it bein illegal. These men essentially lost their lives cuz some horny teen girl cudnt control herself.

User818816
WOW. U r something else. An incel maybe? Never touch a girl in your life? (Consensually nyway)

User61666
Touched plenty u fuckin slag

User818816
You already called me that. Hav u lost ur thesaurus?

User61666
Ur just jealous of her cuz ur too fugly to even be raped.

User818816
Oh u got me u wiley fella u! I sit around desiring rape by virgin misoginystics who spend their time abusing teen victims online. Please, bring me ur tiny cock, I'm gagging 4 it.

User61666
U fkin wish u fridgid bitch

User818816
Thought I was a slag? How can I be a frigid too? (Frigid has no d btw – just like u) Or have u stumbled on the 'antonym' section of the thesaurus?

User61666
Fair play u r fkin borin me now.

User818816
Guess u got 2 be PornHub to keep ur attention

User61666
U fukin wish u cud be fit enough 2 be on Phub

User818816
Oh how well u no me

User61666
Fk u

User818816
Not today thanks mate

[User818816 blocked]

CHAPTER TWENTY-THREE

The hour was growing late, and the full moon appeared bigger than normal. Kevin shut his curtains, hiding the peaceful night sky from his dark office, and sat close to his antique wooden desk, scrolling through the transcript of his conversation with Briony, reading the words over and over and hoping they would offer a different perspective.

Anything so he did not have to arrest her.

It would not look good. The press would hound them. And her. Regardless of what restriction they tried to place on the press, her name had already gone viral on social media—everyone knew who she was. If he arrested her, her life would change. The public would villainise the police for arresting her, but once they learned of the details of the case, they would villainise her instead. Call her a psycho. Ask how a young girl could be so sick. There would be Channel 5 documentaries about her, books written, podcasts discussing her case—it was a bizarre case, and that would illicit the fascination and notoriety that such unusual cases attracted.

Briony's life had already changed so much because of the trauma she'd experienced—but right now the world saw her as a survivor. An arrest and the release of information about the nature of the man's death would change that view drastically.

He might ruin a victim's life.

But a victim doesn't torture people. Only a villain does.

He sighed. Ran his hands through his grey hair. Lifted his head back and stared at the ceiling fan. It span round and round, rotation after rotation, never changing its course.

"What's the matter?"

His wife's voice made him jump. Then it made him smile. It was always a welcome voice; one that gave him a hit of dopamine, regardless of how many years he'd heard it. It was the only voice that calmed him, and the more time he spent at the station, the more he missed it.

He'd promised her he would retire early. They had the money for it. They'd buy a caravan, go away somewhere, maybe the south of France, or on a sunny beach in Spain. But she'd known he wouldn't be able to leave so easily. She'd known he was as married to his career as he was to her. And she'd never held it against him.

"Tough case," Kevin answered.

She walked in and placed a cup of herbal tea on his desk. He held it between his palms and let it warm his hands. She always knew what he needed.

"Tell me about it," she said, moving a stool beside him. She rested her hand on his arm and her head on his shoulder. No part of his job was ever confidential with her. She was the one who listened to his thoughts without judgement, and he needed that.

"It's the same girl from a few weeks ago," he said.

"The one who made you think of how our daughter might have been?"

"Yes. Her. Except, I'm not so sure our daughter would have been like this."

"Did someone hurt her again?"

"It would appear so."

"Then why does this one feel so different?"

What a question.

It was *the* question.

And she knew to ask it.

He kissed her on the forehead and said, "I'm not so sure it's self-defence, and I think I'm going to have to arrest her for murder."

She sat up and appeared perplexed. "Who did she murder?"

"The forty-two-year-old man who groomed her and raped her."

"I don't understand. How does an eighteen-year-old girl become the perpetrator in that scenario?"

"That's what makes it so difficult."

"But he was a predator–"

"Yes, but—maybe so was she."

Janine took a moment to consider this. Kevin wanted to hear what she thought—she was the reason to his rhyme, and it was her words that so often brought him the most wisdom.

"How?" she asked.

"She didn't just kill him and run out—she tortured him."

"And what does your gut tell you?"

He said nothing for a moment, trying to listen to his gut, trying to hear what it had to say. "That she's eighteen and he was forty-two," he answered.

"There you go then."

"But also that there is more to this than the obvious."

She tilted her head. Took a deep breath and let it go. "What is it you used to say when you first started investigating, all those years ago? That saying you had, do you remember what it was? Go where… What was it? Go where…"

"Go where the evidence goes."

She smiled and it made his belly flutter.

His phone rang.

"It's probably work," he said.

"Understood." She stood up and ran her hand over his shoulder. "Don't stay up too late."

"I won't."

She paused in the doorway and said, "I love you."

"I love you too."

She closed the door and he answered the phone.

"Hello?"

"Kevin. It's Beatrice."

"Beatrice. How can I help you?"

She sniffed. It sounded like she was crying.

"It's Briony, I just… She hasn't spoken since she came home from school yesterday. She won't say a word to me. She's shut herself away. I don't—I don't understand what's happening."

"That sounds like a difficult situation."

"Kevin, can you… Can you tell me what happened in that hotel room? Please. I need to know."

"You know I can't."

"Kevin, I need to understand what is happening with my daughter. What did she do?"

He explained to her that he couldn't say. That he was doing his best to help. That he was investigating it as best as he could, and when the time was right, he could give her more information.

But not now.

Not yet.

"Well then, could you—could you talk to her?" she asked.

"Me?"

"Yes. You're the only one who knows what she went through, she might listen to you."

"Beatrice, I don't know…"

"You said you would. You said you'd talk to her if she needed it."

"That was before… before the latest incident."

"Just a conversation. Go to the park. Walk around. Half an hour. For me. Please."

He huffed. Glared at his police badge that sat neatly on the desk.

"If what happened between us meant anything to you, then you'd do it."

He said it wasn't a wise idea.

That he shouldn't talk to a vulnerable girl alone.

That he didn't want it to impact the decisions he had to make.

That he shouldn't go against what's best for the investigation.

That he didn't think his colleagues would approve.

Then he agreed to meet her at two in the afternoon.

He wasn't the hardened police officer he once was. He was getting older, and his empathy had grown too strong. All he wanted to do was help.

He just hoped it wasn't a decision that he would regret.

Unfortunately, it was.

CHAPTER TWENTY-FOUR

The park was empty. It was a cloudy day, and whilst the occasional mother walked by with a stroller or a pre-school child, Kevin and Briony were undisturbed.

From the moment he'd picked her up, he knew it was a bad idea.

It was something about the way she looked when he suggested a walk in the park. The way she stared at him for a little too long. The way the park seemed to elicit a strange smile that looked out of place on her face.

It made him wonder if there was something significant about the park. Whether she'd been there with her mother, or played there as a child, or fed the ducks in happier times. She wandered around aimlessly with him, a comfortable silence hanging between them, always walking slightly behind.

He found a bench. Sat down. She sat beside him and shot him an odd look. He realised it was because he was staring at her. He couldn't help it. He felt guilty. His police force had failed to protect her. She used to be fragile like a breeze, and now she was furious like a storm. He felt responsible for the person she had become.

He recalled something his old inspector had said, back when he first joined the force—an old-fashioned, stuffy man with a big moustache who'd retired to Portugal and died a few years ago. He'd always said that to defeat a monster, one must become a monster. Kevin thought he was talking about being a good police officer, but he wasn't. He was talking about how a victim became an assailant. And although Briony hadn't any claws or scales, or the vile inclinations of the sadists who'd groomed her, she was already blurring the lines of right and wrong, and was struggling to stop herself from becoming the monster she was becoming—he was determined not to exacerbate her deterioration further by needlessly arresting her. He needed the truth, and the conversation he was about to have with her was the only solution he could think of, and the thought that it might not work terrified him.

"How are you doing, Briony?" he eventually said, breaking the silence.

"Fine."

"Do you know why I brought you here today?"

She shrugged. "I don't know. Most men don't bother—they just want to go straight to the hotel room."

It was a strange comment, and the more he dwelled on it, the more concerned he became that she was misconstruing this entire situation. Wishing to tackle any misunderstandings, he quickly said, "I'm here to help you, Briony; not take you to a hotel room."

She smiled. It was strange. Slightly demented, whilst also quite childish.

"Your mother's worried about you," he said.

"You're friends with her, aren't you?" she retorted.

"I think so, yes."

"How does Dad feel about that?"

"I don't know, Briony, how should he feel?"

Another shrug. "I'd find it strange for her to have male friends."

"A woman can have male friends without there being something else to it."

"No. She can't."

She was so stiff in how she made that statement. So resolute. So determined that she was right.

"I want to help your mother, Briony. That's why I'm talking to you. And I want to help you."

She turned her legs toward him until their knees touched. He flinched away, then instantly regretted the reaction. It seemed to make her smile again, and she did not move away.

"I'm worried about what these experiences are doing to you. Mentally, I mean. I'm worried that you're getting yourself into a mess that you won't be able to find your way out of."

She placed her elbow on the back of the bench behind him, leant further toward him, and flicked her hair over her shoulder. She rested her cheek on her fist and gazed at him awkwardly. She opened her knees a little.

"They were a similar age to you, weren't they?" she said. "Those men I hurt... I mean, maybe a little younger. But similar."

"That would be the only thing we have in common."

She shook her head. "You're a man. You all have something in common."

"Maybe that's true in some men."

"Do you have children?"

"...No."

"Why did you hesitate?"

"It's not relevant."

"You wanted them, didn't you? But you couldn't."

"Briony–"

"Is she baron, officer?"

He wasn't taken aback.

He'd interviewed the sickest bastards one could ever

know, and none of them had ever made their way into his head. His skull was bullet proof. His mind was protected.

But it did alarm him—why was she trying so hard to provoke him?

"Briony, I am here to help–"

"Why do you keep saying my name? Is it some police technique to form a connection?"

"It's not–"

"Do you want to form a connection with me?"

"As I keep saying, I am here to help you."

"You always are. All of you. Aren't you? Always here to help. Be my friend. Tell me I'm beautiful. Say whatever it takes."

"This isn't like that."

"That's another thing you all say. That you are different. But when I come to think about it, you are all exactly the same."

He looked down at his feet. Took a moment. He could feel her eyes burning into his face, and he tried to look pensive rather than irked. But this wasn't what he expected.

He didn't realise the girl was this far gone.

He thought he could help—but she truly was a victim of her circumstances.

Perhaps he should have taken her to the station—it would have been more professional there. But the station was the scene of her recovery—every time something bad happened, she ended up at the station. It was a place of trauma and sadness. So he'd chosen the park, hoping he could encourage her to talk honestly about what had happened. But she was an enigma. A puzzling catastrophe. Her trust had been betrayed, and whoever she was before was gone—even the best psychiatrists rarely managed to retrieve the innocent person they once were.

He tried a different approach. Tried being blunt.

"Tell me about the crime scene," he said. "Tell me about Charles. About what he did to you."

"He sodomised me, officer."

It was so matter of fact. So blasé. She was so distanced from the words she was saying that she probably didn't understand the impact of saying them.

"I'm sorry to hear that," he told her. "Did that make you angry?"

"Ooh, livid." That damn smile was back again.

"And what did that make you do?"

"All sorts of things."

"If we were to go down to the station, and I were to caution you, would you tell me about those things?"

"How about we go back to a hotel room and I tell you about them there?"

She put her hand on his leg.

He stood. Stepped back. Put an invisible barrier between them and refused to cross it.

"Briony—"

"There's my name again."

"I'm here to help. I'm not here for that."

"It's what you want, isn't it?"

"No."

She whispered, "Liar."

He looked around. A few passers-by aimed glances in his direction. A few cautionary pauses in people's strides. Then the moment passed, and they moved on.

Her words were grotesque, but he'd seen it before—victims of abuse who didn't receive the support they needed, ended up equating sex with love, and spent the rest of their lives seeking unhealthy attachments under the misguided belief that they were being loved and not used. She needed help, but all the state could afford was to give her a crappy school counsellor with a basic mental health qualification who dumped her the moment she seemed okay and their caseload became too great.

And now, Kevin was afraid it was too late.

But he hoped he was wrong.

Oh, how he hoped he was wrong—about so many things.

"I'm going to call your mother to take you home," he said.

"Why won't you take me home?"

"I don't think that's a good idea."

He called her. She said she was on her way. Would be ten minutes. They were a long ten minutes. She didn't stand up, but she didn't stop staring at him either, watching him, considering him like he was a target.

Honestly, he was a little scared.

Which was ridiculous.

This was a young girl.

But he'd seen the crime scene. Seen what she'd done. And now, having witnessed her behaviour, he knew what he was going to have to do.

He would meet with his team in the morning to plan the arrest.

He had no choice.

He kept telling himself that, over and over—*I have no choice. I have no choice. I have no choice*—until, eventually, her mother came and collected her.

He felt relieved. Oh, how he felt relieved. She was a deeply troubled girl who was inevitably struggling to relate to men in a normal way after hugely horrific experiences, and he had put himself in a precarious situation, and he felt stupid for agreeing to something so silly, and he was so, so pleased that it was all over.

He drove home, thinking about how he would handle the situation. He'd have an all-female interrogation team interview her, meaning she would not try to play any of these games. He would watch and listen, but his interactions with her were over.

He would not talk to her again.

Little did he realise, however, that his wallet had fallen out of his back pocket as he'd stood up to put distance between them. Briony had put her foot on it, moved it under the bench, and hidden it there until she left, keeping it out of sight.

He had been so desperate to keep away from her that he hadn't even noticed.

In that wallet was a debit card, two credit cards, twenty pounds in cash, a picture of his wife, a café loyalty card, and a driver's license.

That driver's license had his full address on.

FINAL MESSAGES BETWEEN DCI KEVIN MCCLUSKEY AND BEATRICE SPECTOR

I'm sorry.

It didn't work.

I couldn't get through to her.

Please forgive me for what must come next.

What must come next?

Kevin?

Kevin?

Don't forget what happened between us.

I will tell.

Kevin.

Kevin?

Please?

KEVIN?

CHAPTER TWENTY-FIVE

Daylight descended into darkness, the coos of the pigeon departed for the hoots of the owls, and Briony laid awake in bed, listening to the sounds of the house.

She'd acted like everything was normal all evening. She'd had tea without saying much, listening to her overbearing brother's complaints about whoever had irked him on this particular day, and her mother's passive aggressive comments about how he could manage it better. She'd eaten her peas and eaten her carrots and eaten her potatoes and eaten her chicken. Then she'd sat in the corner of the living room with a thick fantasy book in her lap while her parents watched mindless television shows and her brother's heavy metal music shook the ceiling.

When half-past nine come around, she'd gone to bed without issue. She didn't argue with her parents—she wasn't like Shane—and she was ensuring she did nothing out of character. She brushed her teeth and said nothing when she heard her parents arguing in their bedroom. She passed the open door and wished goodnight to her mother.

Her mother said goodnight without looking up from her phone.

Already, Briony had been forgotten.

She no longer won the attention of her mother with a simple act of self-defence. She had to go harder. Choose a better target. Choose a better method.

The time on her alarm clock passed midnight and she heard her brother's door close. Her parents had gone to bed earlier without prompting Shane to obey his bed time. It wasn't worth the fight, so they didn't bother. When things were tough, her parents chose apathy.

She waited to hear if his door opened again. After a period of silence, she decided it was safe.

She pushed the covers back, slowly to avoid making noise —she knew she wouldn't wake anyone up with the shuffle of her duvet, but her mission was too important to take even the slightest of risks. She placed her feet on the carpet, softly, the tufts of carpet pricking the bottom of her bare feet.

She'd left her clothes over the back of her chair, ready for this moment. She had a pair of black leggings, a black t-shirt, and a black hoodie. She planned to blend in with the night, and hoped the shadows would conceal her movements. She put each item on delicately, pulled her black bag over her shoulders and tightened the straps, then tiptoed to the door.

She paused.

Listened.

Placed her hand on the handle. Turned it. Opened the door slowly to silence the creak. A quiet squeak responded, and she paused again, ensuring that there were no voices or footsteps. Once she was sure, she closed the door behind her.

She proceeded with stealth. Across the landing. To the stairs. Hands on the banister. One step at a time. Careful. Precise. Stepping lightly. No rush. Got plenty of time.

She did not use the front door. Even at the lightest of use, closing it would shake the house. She couldn't risk it. Instead, she moved through the living room until she arrived at to the big window that gave a full view of the driveway.

She opened it wide. Pushed her leg out. Put her hands on the windowsill. Allowed her toe to meet the driveway. Lifted her other leg over the window pane. Placed her feet together.

She pushed the window closed, gently, then took another moment to listen.

No movement from the house.

Just the rustle of bushes, the distant calls of birds, the occasional passing of a car on a distant road.

She crept along the driveway, tiptoeing, keeping her feet light until she left her family's property and turned down the pavement.

She put her hands in her pockets. Hood up. Eyes ahead. Walked. Turned her walk into a stride. Kept going.

She passed nobody.

It was a strange feeling, being the most threatening person in the night—it was so engrained in her to fear the dark, to fear the man she might cross, so aware of what they could do to her, how they could overpower her, how she could end up the victim of an assault the Crown Prosecution Service couldn't prove.

But tonight, she was the threat.

She was the one who could do things.

She was the reason to be feared.

She took out the police officer's driver's license and laughed at his stupid picture. No one looks good in these photos.

She took her phone from her pocket and put his address on her maps app.

It said that it would take her half an hour to walk.

She'd be there in less than twenty.

CHAPTER TWENTY-SIX

Kevin relished the tranquillity of a gentle night; it gave him a mental clarity that stormier nights didn't bring. The breeze was a calm whisper, the clouds were sparse and slow, and the serenity of the night was beautifully apparent.

He arrived home late with the expectation he would leave early. There was little else he could do by staying in the investigation room overnight—the evidence was being processed, the interrogators were preparing their questions, and the crime scene was being guarded. Besides, he was going to need to rest for the morning. Arresting an eighteen-year-old victim of abuse was not a decision he had taken lightly, and he was going to need all the energy he could to manage his colleagues and deal with the media.

It was going to be a long, tough day.

As he heated his wife's night time glass of milk on the stove, he recalled the days in his twenties when he wouldn't even go home between shifts. He'd keep going, only popping home temporarily to bring dinner to his pregnant wife. He couldn't imagine having such levels of energy now.

The memory of his pregnant wife made him smile. They

were so hopeful, so excited about what was to come. In a strange way, he considered them fortunate—rather than growing apart as many couples might, their love for each other grew stronger with every horrible experience they endured—but there was still something missing; a gap in their life they both felt. A savings account with no one to save for. A spare room with a cabinet full of bills and drawers full of old Christmas cards. A space on their three-seater sofa that would never be filled.

That space would always remain empty, and that was something he'd come to terms with long ago.

The milk began to boil. He poured it into a glass, locked the front door, and plodded upstairs. He found his wife in bed, reading a book. Dickens, by the look of it. He smiled at the sight. She was the only person he knew who read the same Victorian literature over and over and over, refusing to even acknowledge today's book charts.

"Here you are," he said as he placed the glass on her bedside table.

"Thank you," she said, lifting her lips for a kiss which he happily gave.

He climbed into bed, turned his bedside light off, and lay down.

"Is my light disturbing you?" she asked.

He'd fallen asleep whilst she continued reading every night for the past thirty-five years, yet she still asked if he wanted her to turn out her light.

"No, it's all right," he said. "You enjoy your book."

He closed his eyes and tried to think about nice things, hoping his mind would travel into the distant lethargy of sleep.

His mind, however, would not comply.

No matter how much he tried to think of Janine, or upcoming holidays, or imminent retirement, his active mind brought his thoughts back to the girl. Briony. Tomorrow's arrest. The questions that would be asked. The answers he couldn't give. For all the decades he'd been doing this job, destroying a person's life had never become any easier, regardless of what they'd done.

He felt movement beside him. He turned over. Janine was out of bed.

"Are you all right?" he asked.

"Just getting some more milk."

"Would you like me to—"

"No, you rest. I can get it."

She left the room. He watched her enter the darkness of the hallway, listened to her soft steps on the stairs, then turned to the empty space in the bed next to him. He could smell her shampoo on the sheets. He closed his eyes, breathed it in, and drifted off.

It was around an hour later when he opened his eyes and realised his wife still hadn't returned.

"Janine?"

He lifted his head. Looked around the bedroom. Scanned the dark corners. Nothing.

The bedroom door was still open.

"Janine?" he said, a little louder.

He sat up.

Listened.

Silence.

"Janine, are you there?"

Listening.

Still listening.

Silence.

Eerie, empty silence.

He sat up. Rubbed his eyes. Pulled the duvet back. Turned his body so his feet landed on the carpet. Ran his hands through his thinning hair. Stood. Opened the curtains.

The night wasn't so calm anymore.

It wasn't ferocious, but it wasn't the epitome of tranquillity it had been earlier. A few specs of rain struck the window, the moon hid behind grey clouds, and a few pieces of litter danced on the wind in the middle of the street.

He edged across the room, listening intently, and paused in the bedroom doorway.

"Janine?"

Nothing.

"Janine, are you there?"

Still nothing.

He peered down the hallway to his right. The bathroom was empty. The spare bedroom was empty.

To his left. Their reading room. Empty.

He used the banister to guide him toward the stairs. Placed his foot on the top step. Listened to the silence. Wary. Worried.

"Janine?"

He continued down, step by step, his heart beating quicker than his body moved.

Artificial light poured out of the kitchen doorway, the amber glow of a cheap bulb.

When he reached the bottom step, he paused again.

Listened again.

Watched the doorway.

There was movement.

It was small, and it was slight, but it was definite. The flicker of a light. The twitch of a body. The stretch of a limb. Someone was there.

He resisted the impulse to shout for his wife, instead remaining calm, creeping across the hallway toward the open door, watching the empty space, waiting for what came, ready for it, to fight any intruder despite his ageing years, to protect his family at all costs.

He wanted to run. To burst in and scream. To lift his fists and launch himself inside. But he needed to think. Be careful. Be still. Be ready.

He reached the door.

Edged into the room.

There was no one standing there.

But a murmur from the floor caught his attention, and he lowered his eyes to those of his wife.

On her front, on the floor.

A ball gag in her mouth.

Her hands and ankles hogtied behind her back.

And Briony Spector knelt over her, a knife in her hand and the blade against Janine's throat.

She grinned at Kevin.

He stared, trying to stop his thoughts from racing, trying to think methodically.

One flick of her wrist and Janine was dead.

The girl was in complete control.

CHAPTER TWENTY-SEVEN

Rage was beauty. Rage was ugly. Rage was real.

And she relished the sight of fear she provoked. The way the police officer recoiled, the way his eyes widened and his pupils dilated, the way his body stiffened and he ceased to move, how his eyes watered, how his breath stuttered, how his usually powerful grimace deteriorated into a feeble contortion—it made her feel important. In charge. In command. In authority.

And having spent a lifetime being repressed, Rage devoured every moment of being alive.

She was Medusa. She was The Morrigan. She was The Deviless.

She was what society creates when a woman is subjected to evil; what happens when patriarchal oppression fails; what occurs when inhibitions and physical strength are no longer barriers to the aggression of the scorned. There would be no more blokes shouting lude comments out of their vans about her school uniform; no more men stroking her bum in a queue and claiming she'd felt something that didn't happen; and no more police officers who thought they were more rational and important than a meek little woman.

There was nothing more important than Rage.

Rage was never weak. Rage never shrank in the face of opposition. When enablers grew more powerful, Rage only grew stronger. Rage would allow no reprieve in the slaughter of violent men.

"Please," he said, his voice shaking, his lip quivering. "Please, you don't need to hurt my wife."

She pressed the tip of the blade a little harder against Janine's throat.

Janine cried. Kevin winced. Rage smirked.

"What do you want?" he said. "Is it money? Is it someone to believe you? Is it–"

"Shut up."

He'd know it was none of those things.

He'd seen what Rage had done.

He'd stood agape at the crime scene.

There was no money that would satisfy Rage. She did not need to be paid. She did not need his diplomatic words.

He was going to attempt to manage her, to talk her down, to use every technique he'd learned through decades of dealing with monsters. But his words would not work. There was nothing he could offer her that she would want; what she wanted had to be taken.

"Fine," he said, his voice low and calm. "If you want me to shut up, then fine. You're in control here. You decide what happens next."

Ah, perfect. It was police negotiation 101. He had the handbook memorised, and he was on the first step—control. He was making sure she knew she had the power, that her next actions were her decision, that she was dictating what happened. Even if he didn't believe it, he had to say it.

"So what is it you want to do here? Because no one has to die, Briony. It's up to you. Entirely up to you."

Next step—use their first name. Become familiar. Make it

seem personal. It was like he was exorcising a demon, and knowing its name gave him power.

But he got her name wrong.

And these tactics did not work on Rage.

"So it's over to you, Briony." He held his hand out in a calming manner. "What do you want to happen next? Do you want to hurt us? Or do you want to reconsider?"

Questions.

Questions, question, questions.

Lots of them.

Make her think. Make her reflect on her actions. Make her understand.

But it just made her laugh.

"I would like you to shut up," she said. "And I would like you to stop being such an unbelievably annoying cunt."

"Look, I–"He stepped forward with his hand out.

"Do *not* fucking move!"

She dragged the tip of the blade down his wife's back, drawing a line of blood, forcing her to scream out for her husband —then she returned the blade to Janine's throat and glared at him.

He held his hands in the air and backed off, increasing the space between them and losing what little ground he'd gained.

"If you try coming toward her again, I'll gut her," she told him. "You've seen what I can do, haven't you?"

He paused, recalling images of a man who'd had his intestines pulled out through his arsehole, and nodded. His cheeks glistened.

"You think I give a fuck about her?" Rage asked. "You think I won't hesitate?"

"I know. You're right. You're in control here, Briony. I won't come any closer."

More techniques.

How pitiful.

"You are going to listen carefully," she said. "And you are going to do everything I say."

"Okay, I will. You just tell me what you want."

"You're going to shut the fuck up for a start."

He nodded. Kept his hands in the air. Failed at holding back tears.

"You will go back upstairs to your room," she said.

He flinched. He didn't want to leave Janine. He wanted to stay, wanted to argue, wanted to remonstrate—but he knew cooperation was the only way to keep them alive.

For now, at least.

"You will sit on the chair in your bedroom. You will tie your ankles to the legs of the chair. You will then handcuff your hands behind the chair. Do you understand?"

"I understand. And then what, will you let her go?"

"This is not a negotiation—this is an instruction."

"Okay. I understand."

"And listen to me very carefully—if I hear so much as a hint of a siren in the distance, or hear movement outside the front door, I will cut your wife's throat. Do you understand?"

"Yes."

"It is imperative that you understand, so I am going to repeat for clarity to ensure that you know your wife's fate lies in your hands—I will slice her throat and watch her die. Do you understand, Officer McCluskey?"

"Yes, Briony. I understand."

"Go. And call for me when you're ready."

He nodded. Backed up.

Looked once more at his wife.

They held their stare. It was only a moment, but they held it.

Rage wasn't sure what he was trying to communicate—reassurance, perhaps? Love? Goodbye? Whatever it was, Rage's hardened glare prompted him to hurry, and he backed out of the room. She listened for his footsteps going up the stairs and into the bedroom. Moments later, she heard duct tape.

She lowered herself down until her eyes were inches from Janine's.

"You think he's going to save you, don't you? That his cooperation will ensure you survive? That he is a good, noble man?"

Janine stared back, wide-eyed, unsure how to respond.

Rage stroked Janine's thick, grey hair and reminded her, "There are *no* good, noble men, Mrs McCluskey."

She flexed her fingers around the handle of the knife and kept its blade pressed against Janine's throat. She moved her mouth to her captee's ear, grimaced at the faint whiff of old-lady-shampoo, then whispered, "And I'm going to prove it to you."

CHAPTER TWENTY-EIGHT

K evin intended to obey every single request.

Every one of them.

Even though he knew it would probably be for nothing.

He'd seen enough home invasions and murders and robberies to know that obeying one's assailant doesn't mean they will grant mercy—just that their victim's death is postponed. But even if it doesn't give a victim a considerable chance, it gives them more chance than if they didn't cooperate. So he obeyed.

For now.

He listened carefully for movement from downstairs. A scream. A cry. A clatter. Something. Anything that would tell him if his beloved wife was still alive.

There were no such noises, and he couldn't decide whether this was a bad thing.

He approached the chair that Briony had spoken of. It was old, wooden, and had Janine's clothes draped over it. They rarely used this chair as a chair, but more of a storing ground for clothes that had been worn but weren't ready to go in the wash yet. He scooped up a pile of shirts and trousers and dumped them on the bed.

He took a tool box from under the bed. Opened it. Took out the duct tape. He stretched it, making sure it was loud, ensuring she would hear and assume he was cooperating.

He also took a pair of sharp scissors from the box before pushing it back under the table.

After opening the cupboard, he took out his uniform, along with his police belt. Removed his cuffs. Put the uniform back in. Then sat on the chair.

He pushed the handcuff key and the scissors underneath the wooden seat of the chair, ripped off a large piece of duct tape with his teeth, and stuck them in place. He ripped off another large piece and stuck it over them again, reinforcing it, ensuring they did not fall off. Then he placed his mobile phone just under the bed and sat down.

Just in case.

He was relying on her not searching the underside of the chair. If she did, he was screwed. But this wasn't a clever criminal—this was a reckless girl. It was a calculated risk he was willing to take.

Once he was sure the scissors and key were secure, he began following her instructions.

He rolled the tape around his ankle and the chair leg a few times, then ripped it off before doing the same with his other ankle. He put his hands through the loop in the back of the chair and cuffed them together.

For a moment, he sat there, looking around at the room he'd spent so many nights in, holding his wife, kissing her forehead before they slept, making love as the windows steamed up.

This bedroom would be forever tainted.

If they survived, this would always be the room where he was tied up and tormented. It would be the room where he was humiliated and came close to death. It would be the room where the worst moments of his life occurred. And despite this room having been the room they planned to grow old in, it would no longer have the same loving serenity it previously had.

With a sigh, and a hope that obeying her wasn't an incredibly stupid move, he called out to her.

"I'm done!"

There was no response. Not at first. Just silence.

No screams from his wife, no movement, nothing.

"I said I'm done!"

He listened. Hoped to hear his wife's voice. Even if she spoke words of terror, he wanted to know she was still alive.

But he received no such comfort.

After the silence lingered on and his thoughts suggested the worst, he heard footsteps on the stairs, heavy but steady, getting louder until he heard the same footsteps on the landing.

Her shadow approached the doorway. It was a small shadow, petite and without menace, but he dreaded it nonetheless.

She appeared in the doorway. Her hair was greasy with sweat. Her body was hunched over. Her eyes were empty and demented. She surveyed his captive state, examining him, ensuring she was satisfied.

"Is she alive?" he asked.

She didn't respond.

She walked in, not looking him in the eyes. Instead, she pulled on his ankle. Then the other. Then pulled on the handcuffs to check they were secure.

"I did as you asked. Now please just tell me, is she alive?"

Briony turned to the bed where Kevin had left the duct tape. She picked it up and stretched it out as far as it would go.

"Briony?"

She wrapped another few loops around each ankle.

"Please tell me, Briony—I'm cooperating, I just need to know."

She wrapped the duct tape around his torso and biceps. She did this a few times until his arms were constricted and his chest felt tight.

"Please, Briony, just tell me—is she alive?"

Briony wrapped the tape around him a few more times. It felt hard to breathe, but he wasn't sure if this was from the tightness of the tape, or from his anxiety that she wasn't answering his question.

"Dammit, just tell me, is she alive?"

Anger didn't work either. It just made her laugh.

He bowed his head, twisted his face into an ugly grimace, and ground his teeth together.

"Please..." He was crying. He sounded pathetic, and he hated himself. "I did as you said, I just want to know if she's alive."

Briony took out her knife. Inspected the blade. Twisted it in front of her eyes, one way and then the other. She placed it on the bedside table.

It had blood on it, but not much.

Did that mean she hadn't cut Janine's throat?

Or did that mean she'd cleaned the blade?

She threw her hair back, tossing it over her shoulder, turned to Kevin, and finally met his eyes with hers as she spoke.

"Let's begin."

CHAPTER TWENTY-NINE

Kevin had faced burglars. Crack addicts. Gang members.

He'd faced angry husbands with heavy fists, manic wives with sharp knives, and parents with violent tempers.

He'd watched a man slit his own throat, a woman get squashed by a train she dove in front of, and he'd plugged his nose to hide the foul odour when he discovered the body of a man who'd hung himself a month earlier.

There had been incidents where he'd been one-on-one with a group of teenagers with Stanley knives. There had been fights where he'd been surrounded, waiting for backup to arrive, wondering how they'd tell his wife how he died. There had been moments where he'd asked an angry man with a weapon what was troubling him, and the aggressive monster before him had crumbled to his knees and cried.

He'd been punched more times than he could count. Knocked out several times. Saved from a stabbing by his stab-proof vest.

Janine had cleaned his injuries, listened to his stories, and hugged him as tears dampened his cheeks—without ever asking if he was sure he wanted to do this job.

Because she knew the answer.

There was nothing that could have saved him from the life he'd chosen, and he was only a few years away from his retirement party and all the leisure time that came with it. But he would never get to buy their caravan, or their cottage, or their farm. Because this was how he was going to die.

Tied to a chair while his wife was downstairs, possibly dead, hopefully not.

After all the formidable opponents he'd faced, it was going to be a teenage girl that ended him, angry at what had been done to her by men who should have known better. All men were monsters and rapists to her, and he was sad about what they had made her become.

But he was still going to do everything he could to avoid dying today.

"Why did you say no?" she asked, gazing out of the window with her back to him, like a poor imitation of an evil genius in a bad action movie.

"No?"

"You pretended like you didn't want me."

"Oh, Briony. I am sorry that–"

"Do not patronise me!" She turned around and jabbed her finger in his face. "Do not *oh Briony* me—you are not my father, and I am not a little child!"

Kevin nodded. Whatever he had to do to keep her happy. "You're right, Briony. I'm sorry."

"Now answer the question."

He hesitated. He wanted to say it was because he didn't want her, but he felt it would make things worse. Perhaps he could say it was because he was married. Because she was too young. All the logical things that bad men had made her unable to understand.

"Because you're a child, Briony," he said in a soft, dulcet tone. "And I'm an adult. And despite what some men have done, it is not okay."

She shook her head. "Wrong."

She marched across the room. Folded her arms. Leant against the chest of drawers that contained his wife's underwear and his trousers.

"Why do you think it is?" he asked.

She licked her lips as she scowled. "It's not because you don't want me. It's not because you think it's wrong."

"Why don't you tell me why you think it is?"

She took a few strides until she was standing over him. Her sweat glistened in the moonlight. She stank like cheap perfume. She was wearing a lot of it.

"Because you want the world to think that you don't like teenage girls," she told him. "You want to pretend you're different."

"It isn't normal for men to like teenage girls."

"Don't lie. Porn sites are full of them. Teen girl does this, teen girl sucks that, a group of guys fucks this teen girl. You all fantasise about it, you just like to pretend you don't."

"Porn is not real life, Briony."

"Every man I've come across–"

"You've come across bad men, Briony."

She placed her hands on his shoulders. Leant over him. Her hair dangled over his face, imprisoning them together. He could smell mint on her breath.

"You are all bad men," she said. "You just hide it. On the internet, in hotel rooms, in text messages. You walk around like you're not, but you all are."

Her voice was breaking. Like she was holding back tears. Her words were destroying her; she was admitting something to herself that she didn't know she felt. It was tough. She hated it. Kevin could tell. And this could be his way out.

"I understand why you might think that, Briony. I really

do. You have come across some really bad men who have done some really bad things—and they got what they deserved. But not all men are like this."

She laughed. Her eyes were still watering, but she fought it, and she chuckled, and she sneered, and she repeated quietly, as if to herself: "Not all men…"

"That's right, Briony. Not all men."

She shook her head. "You don't get it."

"I'm sorry, Briony, but I love my wife. I think you're a lovely, if troubled, girl—but I am not what you think I am. I am not turned on by you."

"You are really adamant about that, aren't you?"

"Yes, Briony, I am."

"Why don't we test it?"

He frowned. He wasn't sure what that meant.

She undid his belt. Undid his trouser button. Unzipped his flies.

"Briony, what are you doing?"

Pulled his trousers down his legs.

"Briony, don't do this, what are you doing?"

Slithered his underwear down his legs and allowed his podgy dick to flop over his grey pubes.

"Briony, please…"

She wrapped her hand around his dick. Firmly, but not uncomfortably. It felt warm. Her soft skin against his ageing penis.

He had Viagra pills on the bedside table. He'd needed them for a few years now. Janine had hated it at first—she thought it was because of her; that her ageing body wasn't what it used to be; that the wrinkles and folds were more prominent than they'd once been. He'd reassured her it wasn't her. That he still thought she was beautiful. That touching her body was as exciting as it was when they first met; that he loved every part of her, but his body just didn't work like it had when he was young.

But there was no trouble now.

His dick grew, and he felt it expand against her palm, pressing against her fingers, until his erection rose high, tall and stiff, standing to attention like a proud veteran.

"Not all men, huh?" she said.

CHAPTER THIRTY

The noises.

Oh, the noises.

Janine laid on her front, her breasts squashed against the kitchen tiles, her hands and feet firmly hogtied behind her back. She stared at the crumbs beneath the oven. Smelt the ammonia of her kitchen floor cleaner. Grimaced from the pain of the solid surface pushing hard against her chin, her shoulders, her pelvis.

Everything was uncomfortable, from the stretch of her limbs bound behind her, to the cut on her back, to the hardness of her bones against the floor, to the odour of cleaning products.

But nothing was as uncomfortable as the noise.

The girl sounded like a poor imitation of a sex scene in a movie: the overzealous *uh* on each thrust, the unrealistic pleasure of penetration, the manufactured eroticism of an awkward experience. The noises were nothing like sex was; they were how she thought sex should be.

Janine wondered if the noises were for her benefit. Whether the girl was exaggerating them to torment her. Whether they were a demonstration of dominance, an example of what she could take, of what she was entitled to have.

But it didn't make Janine jealous. Because she knew her husband. She knew his soul, his nature; he was not interested in teenage girls. So she didn't believe it.

Didn't trust it.

Her husband's honour was indestructible. He was faithful to the last. He was never erratic, rarely angry, and always calm. There was nothing about those noises that made her think her husband was involved in them.

The hyperbolic screams eventually grew to a crescendo, a grand performance, as poorly faked an orgasm as anyone ever heard. Then they stopped. Silence pursued. And Janine waited.

To die. To live.

She didn't know.

She just waited.

She watched the timer on the oven. Kept track of how long she'd been there. It felt like hours, such was her aching; but it hadn't been.

Footsteps.

There were footsteps.

Stomps across the hallway.

Then slow taps down the stairs.

The girl was coming.

Janine tried to look over her shoulder at the doorway, tried to shimmy her body so she could see what state the girl was in. Was she hostile? Angry? Vicious?

The girl was none of these things.

Briony bounced in like a child in a candy shop, her body light and floppy, her arms loose. She was wearing nothing but her husband's shirt. His brown one that he loved. He wore it most days. Sometimes, when he was away on trips, or was spending most of his time at work on a big case, she'd put that shirt on the bed next to her so she could smell him.

It was tainted now.

Briony practically skipped to the kitchen cupboards and searched until she found a pint glass. She held it under the tap, poured, then downed the whole thing in one go before releasing a grateful *aah*.

Then she leant against the counter. Watched Janine. Grinning.

It was rubbish.

Nonsense.

Her husband's body would have resisted. She wouldn't get anything out of him to create such moans. He would not be aroused by her. She knew her husband's sexual habits, his wants, his needs. Besides, he needed a Viagra pill before any planned evening of romance. Her husband's body would not have allowed it.

Janine had almost convinced herself of this when she caught sight of Briony's legs, bony and smooth, and saw it. On her inner thigh.

No. It could be anything. Anything at all.

It could be…

She couldn't think of an alternative.

But she still didn't believe it.

She looked away, frowning.

"I know, right?" Briony said, a playful, mocking tone dripping from her immature voice.

Janine looked again. Stared at it. Convinced herself it wasn't.

But she knew what semen looked like.

Even the grand extent of her own cognitive dissonance couldn't argue with what she saw dribbling down Briony's leg.

Briony downed another glass of water, then lowered herself to her knees. She patted Janine on her head and whispered, "He barely lasted a minute."

Janine struggled. Fought. Tried to pull at her restraints.

Tried to scream. Tried to call the girl nasty words she'd always been too polite to utter.

But it only widened Briony's smile and intensified her laughter. This girl was unhinged, and Janine wondered how much torment she would put them through before she killed them.

Briony patted Janine on the head again, ran her fingers affectionately down Janine's hair, then stood. Put the glass back in the sink. Wiped her hands on the tea towel. Gave Briony a wave and bounced back out of the room.

Janine cried out as she watched her go. Struggled against her restraints. Tried to wriggle her way across the room.

But it was futile.

She could do nothing but lie there with her thoughts, and no matter how much she clenched her face, or shook her head, or tried to silence her inner voice, she couldn't—her thoughts would not go away.

She couldn't move. Couldn't occupy her body. Couldn't distract her mind. Her thoughts were all she had.

So she spun through each thought like a roulette wheel, landing on one uncomfortable topic at a time.

What she regretted in life.

How pathetic she felt just lying there.

Why this was happening.

How certain she was that they would not survive the night.

And who her husband really was.

CHAPTER THIRTY-ONE

There was talking coming from downstairs.

Kevin was sure of it.

Voices.

Was it Briony? Was it Janine? Was she alive?

Perhaps Briony was psychotic enough to talk to a dead body like it was real. Or demented enough to have discussions with herself. But it gave him hope. Desperate hope, but hope nonetheless. Janine could still be alive.

It gave him all the motivation he needed to take this opportunity.

His ankles were bound. His torso fixed to the chair. His hands cuffed behind his back. His trousers open, his sticky dick slumped on his thigh. Despite his restraints, he could still lower his hands far enough to reach an inch or two under the chair; enough to reach the edge of the tape.

He had to be careful. Nimble. Slick.

If the keys and scissors dropped on the floor, there would be no way he could reach them. And she'd find them. And she'd know. And this whole attempt at escaping would backfire.

He no longer saw the point in cooperation. He expected to

die, and if he didn't do something soon that his fate would be sealed—all he was doing by entertaining Briony's whims was prolonging the torture that would precede his death—so he had to take his opportunity, and his opportunity was now.

He pulled off the edge of the tape. Not all of it, just the edge, enough for him to push his fingers through and reach for the scissors and keys.

He stroked the tip. Caressed the ring of the keys. Ran his fingers over the scissor handles.

He pushed his fingers a little further in. Fed them through the loop of the keyring. Dragged the keys toward him by scraping them across the chair until the keyring fell completely down his finger.

Pause. No movement. No one coming up the stairs.

He made sure he felt the keyring securely around his finger.

Thought of his wife.

Of his love.

Of his Janine.

And he twisted his hand upwards, reaching toward the keyhole in the handcuffs with the tip of the keys. He found it. He held the key tight between his fingers until he was sure it was all the way in. Straining his wrist even harder, he pushed upwards and twisted the key, slowly, definitely, twisted it until it went all the way and the handcuff popped open.

The urge to cry out with joy was strong, but he had done nothing yet. He'd only freed his hands. The tape restricted the movement of his arms, but he could at least move them slightly. Enough that he could reach under the chair and grab the scissors.

The scissors.

He had the scissors.

Adrenaline burst through him. He was panting. He almost had this.

He pushed the scissors upwards.

Opened the blades.

Placed them over the base of the tape.

And he cut.

He wanted to shout for glory, but it was premature.

Still, he was nearly there.

Nearly free.

He cut through a few inches of the tape, then he cut some more, then he–

"What is this?"

He looked up.

She stood there. Still in his shirt. Leaning against the doorway. A child in adult clothing.

"I thought we understood each other," she said, folding her arms and shaking her head like she was admonishing a child. "I thought you were behaving."

He didn't stop. No point now. He was discovered. He may as well do what he could. He cut again, and again—but whilst he thought he'd cut about a foot through the tape, he'd barely penetrated a few inches. She charged forward, her face a contortion of wrath, and punched him in the side of the head. It was weak, like a little girl's punch, but it was enough to make him dizzy and force him to topple over. He landed, hard, on his side, and he couldn't get himself out of this one no matter how much he wriggled.

She took the handcuffs. Put them back on his wrists. Removed the key. Strutted to the window. Opened it.

"No…"

And she threw them out.

He bowed his head. Defeated. Fucked.

She took the scissors from his hand and snapped the blades together. They were big. And sharp. And they would hurt if she plunged them into his flesh; they would kill if she plunged them into his throat.

But she didn't plunge them into his flesh, or his throat.

Instead, she lowered herself to her knees, with a slow,

sinister, deliberate fury that was far more terrifying than the crazed beast he thought he'd unleashed.

She opened the scissors and held his gaze as she placed the blades on either side of his penis.

"Oh, God, no…"

She stuck out a bottom lip and shrugged. "You've got to be punished."

"I'm sorry, I know, I shouldn't have, I–"

She applied a little pressure. He felt it against the soft tissue, the hardened blade against the cushioned shaft.

"If only you'd have just sat there like a good boy…" "Briony, please, I promise, I'll cooperate–"

"Briony?" More pressure. He screamed. "Briony died in that hotel room."

She squeezed a little more, squashing the sides, and he stared at it—a little more pressure and it was gone—and he felt sick, like he was going to throw up, like he was going to pass out.

"Please… Please…"

She tilted her head and twisted her body toward him. "More."

"Please…"

"I said more."

"Please don't do this, please don't, I promise I'll do anything…"

"That's crap. Give me more."

"Anything you want I'll do it I'll do it I swear anything just name it and I'll do it…"

She looked up. Twisted her lips in thought. Pretended to consider his begs. Then she looked at him and displayed her cocky smirk.

"Nah," she said, and she applied the pressure.

It didn't snip like a piece of string—she had to squeeze the blades together, and it looked like a piece of putty that was expanding, the bellend pushing out of the foreskin like a piece of rubber being squeezed from the bottom, and she tightened her grip, and he screamed and wriggled and screamed and wriggled...

It was a tough piece of meat to get through. She ended up having to use both hands to pull the two holes of the scissor handles together—but once she'd gripped hard enough, her face curling under the strain of the strength required, the blades finally met.

It fired across the room like she'd shot it out of a cannon.

Blood squirted upwards, firing over the bedsheets and the carpet, then gushing and pouring out of the hole that was left.

He threw up.

She stuck her middle finger in his hole and laughed.

He cried.

He rested his head in the lumps of sick and cried.

She rubbed his hair, patronising him with her bloody hand, and stood.

He didn't pass out. He didn't wriggle. He didn't move.

He just screamed and cried.

Screamed and cried.

Screamed and cried.

And she watched.

Smiling.

Sadistic.

Silent.

CHAPTER THIRTY-TWO

Janine preferred the noises before.

They were at least human. And they were coming from the girl.

Now they were her husbands, and they were noises unlike any noises she'd heard him make before. They were screams like a crazed banshee, cries like a frantic hag, and begs like someone in utter desperation. Someone who couldn't take anymore. Someone sinking into despair, unable to find a way out.

She tried to imagine what the girl was doing to him.

Then she stopped.

Her imagination was no place to dwell.

What could a person do to another person that could prompt such feral noises?

It was screeching, it was weeping, it was an extended shriek growing soft then loud then soft then loud. And beneath it were cackles. Demented cackles. Low-pitched, low-volume pleasure from the girl behind all of it.

Janine looked over her shoulder. The door gaped open, leading to the hallway. Could she make it out? If she wriggled really hard, could she make it?

And if she did, what then?

She could hardly stand, could hardly open the front door, could hardly go running into the night. Her limbs remained hogtied behind her, fastened hard.

But she could at least try, couldn't she?

And if she failed? She'd be laid in the hallway, beside the front door, showing an unwillingness to cooperate with the girl.

What would be the punishment?

She heard Kevin's punishment, all right. She heard it all. It echoed down the stairs, filled the house with chaos, with frenzy, with anguish.

But Janine was manic and she couldn't stay still—yet at the same time, she couldn't move.

"Pleeeeasse... pleh... pl...."

She closed her eyes. Thought of sunshine picnics and moonlit walks and holding hands. Took herself to happy times, before the girl had probably been born, back when her husband was her hero and she admired everything about him.

Before he'd been reduced to nothing but noises.

Just noises.

Like dying prey being eaten alive.

Helpless.

Emasculated.

Pitied.

Something reduced to a wreckage, like a ship sunk and still sinking, like an animal caught in a trap.

His screams went high, loud, even louder, something making impact, something impaling him, she imagined knives, blades, nails, open wounds and a fading heart.

Was he dying?

The noises sounded like torture, not death.

Or was it death in pre-production? The pieces of his demise being built? The end of his life, but prolonged and drawn-out, deliberate and gradual, slow and agonising?

She shimmied her body forward. She couldn't lie there anymore and do nothing. Her breasts, squashed against tiles, ached. Her knees, bashing against the floor, throbbed. Her neck, stiffened and raised to stop her chin rubbing against the surface, stung. But still, she tried. Twisted her body. Like a snake with no direction. She twisted it and shoved it from one side to the other, and again, and again, and again, and again, and—it was no use. She'd made it inches, and she was sweating, and her body was tired, and it just hurt, and why oh why oh why oh why can't *the noise upstairs just stop already!*

If it was her pathetic orgasm imitation, or her stupid voice, or her silly little taunts, then fine; she hated it, but she still had the mental fortitude to endure it—it was her husband's agony she couldn't take—her strong, domineering husband—her caring, made-of-rock husband—being reduced to this.

To nothing.

To pittance.

To a weeping wreck.

She hoped it would end, that he would pass out, that she would have a break, surely the girl must be running out of energy, surely she'd need relief soon, surely just surely just surely just–

It continued.

Louder.

Harder.

Higher.

Then lower.

Then higher and lower and everything all at once and *oh my god oh my god oh my god please stop hurting my husband please stop please stop please…*

She wept too. Though she kept it quiet. She didn't want him to suffer more by hearing her cry.

So she wept silently.

Tears fell on the floor. She rested her head on the hard, cold surface and they moistened her cheek. She tried to relax her body, but couldn't.

So she let the tears dribble out.

And she waited for it to end.

CHAPTER THIRTY-THREE

Rage was authority. Rage was insubordination. Rage was power.

Rage was what we all suppress, but only a few become liberated enough to unleash.

Rage is who you are when society can no longer contain you. It is eternal. It is indestructible. It is unfathomable.

It is exposed in what you keep hidden. It is what powers your every move, yet it is everything you deny. It is what you admonish others for; what you try not to acknowledge.

You think you feel Rage. You don't. It's not a feeling. It's an experience. It's a compulsion. It's a war.

It takes place inside of you, and you go through your whole life pretending the war has ended, only showing glimpses of its never-ending conflict. That driver that cut you up. That rude email your colleague sent. That person who didn't say thank you when you let them pass. You know that twinge in your belly when this happens?

It's Rage that you feel.

You keep it small, but it isn't small. It's grand. It's epic. It's indefinite.

And when nature's powerful force prevails, it vomits its

magnificent authority over the world; and no matter how many people sneer or disregard or avoid the compulsion, they cannot deny it—Rage is the only thing this world cannot contain.

And it was Rage that Kevin was subjected to.

Carnivorous, insurmountable, uncontainable Rage.

She untethered herself one piece at a time. Played with her food. Toyed with her prey. Shoved as many fingers as she could into the open wound of his crotch and smeared the blood down Kevin's cheek, leaving lines where her fingers had travelled. Slapped him, not caring that the pain was minimal; the mental torment of humiliation hurts a proud man more than any act of violence. Waved his penis in front of his face, laughed as he squealed, cackled as she placed it in his mouth and he didn't know whether to spit it out or protect it from her.

He didn't pass out. He came close, but he stayed awake. This was how she wanted it. Rage would have no fun if its muse closed its eyes. Any moment he seemed to be drowning, seemed to be losing it, when his eyes fluttered, Rage backed off, let him recover, and ensured that he was present for all that she did.

She took his penis from his mouth. Pressed the perforated end against his face and smeared its juices down his cheek, dragging the spongy tissue down his skin, like in primary school when she'd dip her sponge in red paint and drag it down the canvas.

He screamed like a bitch.

A pathetic little bitch.

He must have known by now that death was inevitable. He must have known he wouldn't survive this. And did he really want to? Could a man find a purpose in their existence without a prick? Could a predator enjoy hunting if it didn't have the teeth to bite into their prey once they caught it?

As she sat on the floor, waiting for him to go through his

latest fight for consciousness, his eyes drooping and his head lolling, she saw something under the bed. A toolbox. Delighted, she took it out, and opened it like a child unwrapping a Christmas present.

There was a hammer. She struck it against the wound and marvelled at his widening eyes.

There was a screwdriver. She stuck it into the hole and twisted it, and his scream grew like she was turning the ignition on a car with a fucked engine.

There were pliers. She took hold of a loose flap of skin and pulled it out of the hole. It had been annoying her, like a loose scab that wouldn't fall off. She made him eat it. He cried, but she made him. Then she pitied him.

This poor man.

Poor, poor man.

Rage looked so innocent. Rage looked so kind. Rage looked like she could be nothing but the victim.

And she was a victim.

Rage was always a victim.

She demanded sympathy from the world, not admonishment.

She was doing a service.

She was doing what the justice system could never do.

This wasn't murder.

Women don't murder.

Women snap. Women defend themselves. Women take a stand. Women protest. Women do what they can.

Only men murder. Only men rape. Only men bring forth Rage from a sweet, innocent girl.

Rage takes the form of a woman when she displays what a man calls dominance.

She surveyed the art she'd made. The picture she'd painted. The wriggling body. The man who refused to pass out.

He was a strong one, Kevin. He knew how to endure pain.

He also knew how to inflict it too.

She knelt. Placed a hand on his cheek. Stroked his weary face.

"Poor boy," she said. And she meant it.

He was a poor boy.

He was suffering. He was moaning. Guttural sounds from deep inside his throat. He was trying to speak, but could no longer bring forth the words to beg.

But she was not finished.

"Don't worry," she said. "You'll be dead by the time anyone else sees you like this."

She stood. She needed the toilet.

She walked to the ensuite, opened the door, and looked back. She smiled. She found it so sweet, so endearing, what a man becomes when he can no longer find a way for his aggression to prevail.

She closed the door—she didn't want him to see her pee. He didn't deserve to.

She sat on the toilet. Closed her eyes for a moment, realising how tired she was. The evening had taken a lot of energy from her. She allowed herself to rest for a minute as piss and shit flowed out of her.

Rage was having a good day.

CHAPTER THIRTY-FOUR

There wasn't much of Kevin left.

His torment had stretched the limit of his mental strength. His mind had little left to give, his voice had little left to cry, and his strength had little left to offer. His life was hanging from his consciousness like a loose bit of skin, ready to fall off and decay.

But he was persisting, refusing to lose awareness, determined to stay present, purely for one reason.

Janine.

He had to make sure she was safe.

Then he could die.

He could fall away like the end of a bad movie. The pain could end and eternal emptiness could prevail. The tips of his fingertips could let go of the pain that kept him living.

He just had to make sure she was safe.

He lifted his head. Listened to the girl. From the bathroom.

She was singing.

It was quiet, to herself, like a child, little and pure. It sounded so innocent. It wasn't. It was sinister, morbid, strange.

He listened to the tinkles hit the bowl and the splashes hit the water, keeping track of what she was doing, how long he had. Minutes, maybe seconds.

Laid on his side, he shuffled along the floor. Every movement was horrendously painful. He just had to persevere. It wasn't long until he could let go.

He shuffled again.

He pushed himself along the carpet by his legs and the movement forced a shot of agony through his vacant crotch every time he did. He tasted blood. Felt an absence below his waist that made him sick.

He could die soon. He could. He'd let himself slip away.

But first, Janine.

He shuffled further. His blood gave him something to slide across, making it easier to slither along the frayed tufts of carpet.

He reached the bed. The phone that he'd placed beneath it waited for him. Without the use of his hands, he shoved his head under the bed. It was too low, and he had to force his head under. The metal base of the bed squashed his ear. But who cared? He didn't need it. What good would hearing be when he was dead?

Janine.

That was all that mattered.

She was worth any bit of pain it took to do this.

The singing stopped. The rip of toilet paper followed. She was almost done.

He shoved his head further under, the pressure of the wire that supported the mattress a constant discomfort against his cheek. He lifted the phone with his tongue. Took it between his teeth. And he dragged his head back out from beneath the bed.

With his nose, he pressed the home button, and allowed his Face ID to unlock it. The phone had to consider it, unsure whether this twisted face was still his, but it eventually complied.

He clicked the phone icon.

Clicked on the keypad.

And he pressed his nose against nine.

Nine.

Nine.

The toilet flushed.

It rang. And rang. And rang.

"Which service do you require?"

"Police."

His voice was broken. There was no response from the other side of the line, and he had to say it again, trying to force his voice out, enough to make it clear, but not enough to be heard from the other side of the bathroom door.

"Police."

It rang.

The tap ran. She was washing her hands.

"Police emergency."

"This is DCI Kevin McCluskey, there is an intruder in my home, she's about to kill us, send–"

The door unlocked.

He hit the end call button with his nose, then shoved the phone back under the bed with his forehead. He shuffled backwards, attempting to return to where he had been, an inch or two away from the bed.

She left the bathroom, barely filling the doorway. This little creature, demented and petite, looked at her prey with a sick grin, curved in a way that made it look unreal.

"What now?" Kevin grunted. "What are you going to do to me now?"

She crouched beside him. Wiped the blood from his eyes. Ran her hand through his hair like she was stroking a pet.

"Oh, Kevin," she said. "You really wanted to change the world, didn't you?"

She sighed. Shook her head like Kevin was foolish. Like he was the twisted one. Like he was a silly, silly sausage.

"I am going to slit your wife's throat," she told him. "Then I am going to set it all up so they think you did it."

She tapped the side of his cheek.

"But we're not finished yet," she said. "You still have so many things I can remove."

She stood.

He stared at the phone beneath the bed. Hidden from her. Unnoticed.

He hoped it was enough.

That they'd find his address in his records and get here urgently.

That they would find their way in and rescue Janine before the girl made it downstairs.

It didn't matter what happened to him now.

His life was over. He was done. He was in the waiting room, waiting for death to arrive.

He was relying on his colleagues now.

The ones he'd often trusted with his life. Who'd obeyed his orders and addressed him with respect. Who'd never let him down before.

He just had to stay awake. Stay aware. Stay conscious long enough to keep her torturing him, to keep her from going downstairs, to keep her from hurting Janine.

It should be a matter of minutes.

Just minutes.

That's all.

Minutes.

Long, strenuous, stretched-out, torturous minutes.

"Come on then, you bitch," he said to her. "Give me all you got."

She had no problem responding to his request.

CHAPTER THIRTY-FIVE

Aching.

Her body was aching.

The awkward contortion of her body had become a dull pain; a prolonged stab of drawn-out anguish.

But the pain kept her alive.

That, and the stark realisation that her husband had stopped screaming.

She'd hated the sound. It had tormented her with images of what could be happening, making her constantly aware of how much he was suffering. Now the silence was louder, and she'd give anything to go back to hearing him scream; at least she'd know he was alive.

She rested her left cheek on the tile floor. Across the kitchen was the open door to the dining room. She could see the brown antique dining table they'd inherited from her mother. It was the same table she'd sat at when she was a child. There had been mornings at that table with squash and croissants and pancakes and laughter. There had been tea times with roasts and pastas and food her mother always attempted but got horribly wrong—they ate it regardless, never wanting to upset someone who tried so hard to keep her family happy. There had been weekends with crayons and paints spread over a stained cloth, pictures and paint-by-numbers and colouring books bought as presents to keep her quiet. She looked so different now compared to the girl who'd sat there and created whatever she felt like creating; life had provided wrinkles to show the struggles she had since endured.

But she'd never return to that age.

Because there were other times at that table, too. Times when she hid beneath it to conceal herself from her parents' arguing. The Sunday evening they sat her down at that table and explained what divorce meant. The table her mother cried at, when she watched her from the stairs after bedtime, when her mother didn't know she was there.

They were supposed to have made new memories at that table.

They were supposed to have given their son or daughter happy moments on those chairs. Then, they were supposed to have passed the table down to them so they could one day stare at it, reminisce, and consider how the grooves and marks stayed the same, but the people who sat at it changed so drastically.

But it hadn't happened. And the table had remained just a table. And the walls had remained just walls, and the spare room had remained a spare room, and the kitchen tiles had become the location of her current suffering.

She closed her eyes. Still, he was silent. Still, there nothing. Only the occasional creak of a floorboard—but that could be anything. Her moving his body. Her ripping apart his body. Her jumping on his corpse.

All thoughts that made her cry.

But she didn't cry.

Why bother?

Crying was for people who could be heard.

She turned her head the other way. Her neck was hurting.

But it didn't relieve the pain. Whichever way she rested her head, it hurt. The pain didn't end. She tried closing her eyes and giving in to fatigue, but all she saw was her husband's dead face staring back at her.

Then there was something…

Faint, but possible…

She lifted her head.

In the distance, she heard it.

It took her a moment to be sure.

Sirens.

But they couldn't be for her. They were too far away. They were for someone else. Someone who could get to a phone, someone who could ask for help. It probably wasn't even a police car.

But the sirens didn't grow fainter. They grew louder.

Still, they could be going past. Could be going to a nearby street. Could be taunting her with the potential of salvation.

But they didn't grow fainter. They became louder, and louder still, until they consumed the street. Outside the window, flashing lights between the curtains, the rotation of the light bar illuminating the room.

The lights and the sirens had stopped outside.

They were here.

They were actually here.

She lifted her head.

There were stomps upstairs. Louder. More frequent.

Had he managed this?

There was movement outside the window.

Bodies.

Uniforms.

"This is the police, open the door!"

No one was opening the door.

The stomps upstairs grew more hurried. More frantic. More frenzied.

She was reacting. She was caught.

If Kevin wasn't dead, would she kill him now?

Would she do it before they got in?

The house shook under the collision of something against the door. A boulder or barrier, whatever it was called—she'd heard Kevin say what they were called, she just couldn't think —but she could think—she could think enough to shout, even if that was all her thoughts could form.

"Help! Help, I'm in the kitchen!"

More strikes.

They were taking too long.

The door wasn't coming down.

Strike. Strike. Strike.

Come on, hurry up.

The stomps upstairs became chaotic. It wasn't just someone walking, it was someone falling, someone doing something to someone or something...

There was the creak of a door coming off its hinges, but not fully, and they kept striking, kept striking and striking and striking.

"In the kitchen!"

More strikes, and the door collapsed, and feet charged through—"Police, make yourself known!"—and they entered a room, and another room—"Clear!"—she lifted her head, "I'm in the kitchen please help"—shadows in the doorway—"We've got one!"

An officer rushed to her side and examined her restraints.

She didn't care about the restraints.

She was fine now.

"My husband is upstairs," she told him.

The police officer turned to the officer behind him and relayed the information.

The officer proceeded up the stairs.

CHAPTER THIRTY-SIX

"What's that?"

Rage lifted her head. There were flashes of colours outside the window. Sirens wailing. Lights filling the street.

She looked down at Kevin, his head resting in a pool of warm blood beside her knees. He made little to no noise. Just gurgled and croaked. She squeezed his chin and twisted his face toward hers. His distant eyes, glazed by persistent tears, lolled to the side. That he was still conscious was bizarre; younger, stronger men would have passed out from the torture. But he was still here.

She stood. Strode to the window.

Police cars. Several of them. Too many.

The house shook. Something hitting the front door.

"This is the police, open the door!"

She turned back to Kevin. But how... It wasn't possible...

His head rested on his shoulder and his distant eyes looked under the bed.

She returned to her hands and knees, shoved her hand beneath the bed, and withdrew a phone.

Rage glowered. Snarled. Shook with fury.

"You…"

Rage tried to contain herself. Tried to quell what it was. Tried to hold back its nature.

"I. Thought. I. Told. You. Not. To. Phone. The. Police!"

Rage grabbed her knife, flexing her claws over its handle, and shoved it into the side of the bastard's neck.

Cutting someone's throat isn't like in the movies. It wasn't so easy. She didn't have the strength to penetrate the muscle. And the thyroid gland. And the trachea. Or larynx. Or oesophagus. Or whatever it was she aimed to penetrate—she didn't give a shit, she hated biology—but she shoved as hard as she could. It forced a squirt of blood like a broken tap, then the knife remained lodged in the side of his neck.

She rose above the knife, placed both her hands on the end, and used all her bodyweight to push it in.

It broke through whatever it was stuck in. She couldn't see what the knife had gone through, it dribbled too much blood, but she didn't care, she just wanted it done, so she pulled the knife across his throat, dragging it with all her strength. A squirt of red assaulted her mouth and she licked her lips. She loved the taste of predator.

He spluttered and gurgled and stared at her with a look of shock only the dead wear.

"I told you not to!"

She pulled the knife out. It was resistant, stuck on whatever it had gone through, but she managed it with a big yank.

"I fucking told you not to!"

She struck the throat again. There was no resistance this time. It went through, prompting another squirt of blood that rose above her and landed on the top of her head.

"I told you didn't I!"

The house shook as the front door broke down.

"I told you!"

She stabbed again. And again. And again.

Though there was no point.

He wasn't moving.

His chest wasn't expanding.

The entire room was a painting of death. It was a master-piece of retribution. A wonder of woe.

"Room clear."

They were in the house.

"Help! Help, I'm in the kitchen!"

She stood. Looked down at the glorious mess that she had made. At a man who'd never had the chance to hurt her.

"In the kitchen!"

She backed up. Opened the window.

There was a tree across the garden.

She could make it.

She knew she could.

Feet pounded up the stairs.

"Hallway, clear!"

Below the tree were police cars. There were a lot of them. Most were empty; she assumed most officers were in the house. A few remained outside. She felt it was excessive, but she understood—Kevin was their leader. They were the biggest gang in the country, and they would send everything they had to protect one of their own.

The bedroom door opened.

"Do not move!"

She leapt.

The probe of a taser hit the wall beside her.

They galloped in.

"We have him! Boss? Boss!"

Cries of anguish followed as they beheld the remains of their detective inspector. A few arrived at the window in time to see Rage crawling down the branches and dropping to the floor.

They used their radio to inform the police outside. She'd sprinted halfway down the street by the time they saw her and gave chase.

She turned into an alleyway.

Some pursued her on foot. Some returned to their cars. The beating of a helicopter's propellors travelled overhead.

They were going to hunt her with everything they had.

She turned down another alleyway. Caught her breath. Wondered what she was going to do. Heard footsteps. Kept running.

She left the alleyway and came across a bike. A bike on someone's front lawn. There were other toys too, and a sign that read *Help yourself.* Such kind neighbours. She tucked her knife down her sock and mounted the bike.

She pedalled with a ferocity that matched her eagerness to escape.

She cried. Tears down her cheeks. Rage had departed, leaving Briony with the terrifying thoughts and the sick memories and the grave burden that came with what she had done.

It's hard to tell why she kept running. She knew she could not escape when they were watching her in the air, and she hadn't thought far enough ahead to consider what would happen if they caught her.

Perhaps she ran because it was all she could do.

The world had created her, and now it must punish her for it.

But if I, as your lowly narrator, had to guess why she ran, I'd say it was because her body compelled her to. So long as she was moving, she didn't have to think about what she'd done. She didn't have to face the images Rage had left in her memory. She didn't have to confront the terror she had created.

So long as she kept moving, she was safe from her thoughts.

For this reason, she would keep running until she could not run any longer.

No one wanted to save her anymore.

ONLINE COMMENTS BELOW NEWS ARTICLE REPORTING ON THE MURDER OF DCI KEVIN MCCLUSKEY

Yeh… only a psycho wud do that kinda shit

Effect of trauma? Fk off! I was traumatised n I don't go clamping blokes arseholes open

What the men did to her was bad. What she did to that man was worse.

Knew all that innocent groomin shit was an act fkin psycho bitch #BitchesBeCrazy #WTF

What. A. Weirdo.

Yeeeeeeeh… u cnt do that to someone, rapist or not
Guy wants to have sex wiv pretty girl. Guy gets his insides pulled through his arsehole. Girl murders cop. #MakeItMakeSense

18 isnt too young to know what guys r like. Women aren't all innocent u no.

I see all the feminists have gone quiet this morning…

Just spittaked my spaghetti. Never going to be eating THAT again.

Innocent girls don't torture men #LetsGetReal

Does anyone no if he actually did anythin? Cuz I heard there were no messages or nothin n she brought this to him
Look up 'overreaction' in the dictionary n youll find this girls picture

#DontBeLikeBriony

Sorry – but what? Sure its weird, but was this the THIRD bloke who did something to her? What did you people think was goin to happen?

Still bitches who still thinkin #BeLikeBriony – if you still think she's all innocent youre deluded.

Feminists – if you condone her actions, you lose all integrity for your cause.

Bet she groomed those blokes too, not the other way round, the psycho beatch

Selfdefence is not torture #MensRights #JusticeForMen
Still want to #BeLikeBriony ?

If she killed them cuz they did some shit to her fine – but she didn't, and I don't know wot they did. She fkin ruined them. This is NOT normal.

She doesnt deserve our sympathy. Not anymore.

Rape is not normal. But this is beyond not normal. FUCKED UP doesnt even come close.

Imagine matching on Tinder with Briony. FML...

Briony – a girl who never gets a second date. LOL.

What the fk her parents bn teaching her? Where they at?

She is not the victim.

Okay feminists, off you go – justify this.

#PervertedLittleFreak

CHAPTER THIRTY-SEVEN

Sweaty. Blood-stained. Exhausted.

Briony pedalled as fast as her legs would manage, each rotation another stab of pain in her calves, another shot of agony up her thighs.

But she couldn't stop.

The sirens were loud. She couldn't see them, but she could certainly hear them. Everywhere and nowhere.

Eyes followed her. Curtains twitched. Noisy neighbours annoyed by the commotion. Annoyed by the interruption to their sleep. Annoyed but fascinated by the show.

Briony wished that it would end, but she knew the police would not stop. She'd hurt one of their own. Another officer. They wanted blood. They would have blood.

She would have whatever fate gave her.

Pedal. Pedal. Pedal.

Uphill, harder.

Turned down another street.

Down another alley.

Back onto the road.

Downhill. Easier. But still hard.

The sirens were inside her head, trapped in her thoughts,

in her skull, in the prison of her mind. They were punching at the bars, bouncing off the walls, waving and spinning around and around and around.

She was dizzy.

Suddenly, so dizzy.

The bike tilted. She fell. Scraped her leg. Dried blood clung to her skin. She wanted to pull it off. The sight of it made her sick. This wasn't her.

None of it was her.

Yet all of it was her.

She pushed the bike back up. Glanced over her shoulder. They weren't behind her, but they were above her. Floating. Watching. Was her body heat making her a green splodge like on those police shows? Was she being filmed? Would they make a documentary about her?

She wouldn't be caught.

She couldn't be caught.

They'd kill her for what she'd done.

Even if they didn't take her life, they'd still kill her. Another psychotic woman in the penal system. Another figure of hatred for the patriarchy. Another example of why women do not deserve sympathy.

She couldn't be what they wanted her to be.

She put her foot on the pedal. On the other. Tried to steady it. Tilted from one side to the other. Gained balance. Pushed on.

Push push push.

Pedal pedal pedal.

Sweat sweat sweat.

She ignored the tears. They were part of her armour now. Her arm was sticky from the ones she'd already wiped away.

Flashing lights past the end of the street. They were searching for her. They were close.

Propellors above. They were guiding them. They were watching her.

She turned down another road. There was a police car up ahead, driving away from her. It screeched to a halt. Turned around, twisting until it faced her, and sped up.

She pedalled toward it.

Played chicken.

Tempted it to hit her.

Wished it to hit her.

Begged it to hit her.

It sped up. Collision imminent. Almost there.

Then it turned and skidded to a halt on somebody's lawn, flattening their flowers and bushes.

Cowards.

She'd done all she'd done, and they couldn't even knock her off a bike.

If she was Ted Bundy, they'd knock her off.

If she was Jeffrey Dahmer, they'd back up and run her over again.

If she was Fred West, they'd be forgiven for doing it.

But she wasn't. She was Briony Spector. She was an eighteen-year-old girl, which meant they didn't even have the compassion to condemn her like they would if she were one of *them*.

She had excuses. So did they. So do we all.

It didn't mean she deserved to live.

She wasn't sure if she wanted to live.

The car spun around and drove after her as she turned the corner and made it onto the main street. It drove behind her, inches from her wheel, and she pulled the brakes, tempting them to collide with her, but they broke too, and she screamed in frustration.

She turned right. Down another street. Pedalled hard. Stopped as she came to a dead end. A high, barbed wire fence. Houses either side, and a factory in her way.

The police car followed her, slowly, not needing to chase

anymore. She remained in its headlights, illuminated by unflattering white beams, sneering at her pursuers.

They stepped out of the car. One of them had a taser. They shouted things at her. She didn't listen.

She stepped off the bike, pulling the knife out of her sock as she did.

"Drop the knife!"

She didn't drop the knife. But she didn't approach them either. And they didn't come any closer. They just stood there, knowing she had nowhere to go. She didn't pose enough of a threat for them to fire the taser—if she was a large man she'd be convulsing on the floor right now, but they didn't even have the kindness to fry her.

More cars pulled up behind them. More officers stepped out. But they just stood there. Like there was a barrier between them. Like there was a no-man's-land that neither of them would enter. Like they were in their trenches, and she was in hers.

"Drop the knife!"

She still didn't drop the knife.

Nor did she threaten them with it.

Instead, she lifted it slowly to her chin and placed the tip of the blade beside her throat.

She'd already slit Kevin's, she could slit hers too. She knew how much force it would take. And with her dainty neck, it would be even easier.

"I have a taser, drop the knife!"

She didn't understand why the police officer felt the need to point out he had a taser. She could see it. It was pointed right at her. And if he was going to use it, he would have used it by now.

"Drop the knife! Drop the fucking knife!"

So impolite. So forceful. So… manly. His big gruff voice telling her what to do, trying to sound as dominant as he could, as authoritative as he could.

But she didn't care.

She didn't want to live.

Not knowing what she had done. Who she was. How they would sell her to the world.

Her time as a hero had ended—she should have done this before she'd let Rage go this far.

"Drop the knife, Briony! Drop it!"

Why would she drop it?

How would she slit her own throat if she dropped it?

Silly fools. Pitiful men. They didn't understand.

She did not care if they kill her.

But she cared if they took her. She cared if they locked her away. She cared if they told everyone she was an evil bitch who proved that women can be cunts too.

"Briony, drop it, now!"

She pressed it harder against her throat.

Closed her eyes.

Flicked her tongue against the roof of her mouth, ready for the glorious taste of her blood.

She could smell the smoke of Hell, could feel its fire, could hear its screams.

She was almost there.

Almost.

Almost…

She opened her mouth. Took what she intended to be her final breath.

Then she heard a voice she didn't expect to hear.

"Briony?"

And she was still.

TRANSCRIPT OF TELEPHONE CALL BETWEEN INSPECTOR ROBERT MARLAND AND BEATRICE SPECTOR

Inspector
Hello Mrs Spector?

Beatrice
Yes.

Inspector
This is the police.

Beatrice
Oh my god (…) do you know where she is (…) have you found her?

Inspector
We need you to come now.

Beatrice
My god is she alive?

Inspector

She's alive but (…) but she's threatening (…) we need you to come (…) she has a knife.

Beatrice

Who's she threatening to hurt?

Inspector

Herself.

Beatrice

Where are you?

Inspector

A police officer is coming to collect you now (…) we need you to talk to her (…) talk her down the best you can.

Beatrice

Why is she threatening to hurt herself (…) what did you do to her?

Inspector

Mrs Spector (…) she has (…) it's best you come and we'll explain.

Beatrice

I see them (…) they are outside (…) I'm coming now (…) just don't let her hurt herself (…) don't let my baby hurt herself (…) please.

CHAPTER THIRTY-EIGHT

"This is your fault."

Briony didn't intend to say these words. It almost wasn't her saying them. But it wasn't Rage—Rage was long gone—it was her, and she said them, and she hated herself for them.

She'd never shown this woman weakness unless it was to illicit her love. Now the shame and fear in her mother's face felt different. It felt raw. Like she was now the victim.

It was Briony that had done that.

It was all Briony.

"Briony, darling–"

"This is your fault."

"How–"

"If you'd have just loved me. Unconditionally. Without me needing to hurt anyone. Then this—this wouldn't have happened."

"Briony, I do love you uncondi–"

"*Liar!*"

Her voice echoed around the alleyway. Every siren was off. Every officer was silent. The remnants of a storm fell from gutters in distant drips.

Other than that, there was just their voices.

Mother and daughter.

The loved and the unloved.

"You never loved me unless you hated me!"

Briony couldn't recognise the spite in her voice. She never shouted. Never spoke like this to her mother.

"Briony, why don't you put the knife down and we can talk about—"

"If I put the knife down, there'll be no way we can talk."

The edge of the knife pricked her throat and a small ball of blood dribbled warmth down her skin.

Her mum hesitated. Wiped her eyes. No mother ever expected to be in this position, but it was her fault. It was all her fault.

Wasn't it?

Briony felt her face twist and contort into the ugliness of sobs. She hated herself for this. She'd expected to go out in glory, with police begging her not to do it, and for her blood to be over their hands.

She had not expected to see Mum.

And everything inside of her was now surfacing, and it felt big, and complicated, and sickly, and manic, and like it wouldn't stop wriggling and screaming and crying.

"You! This is because of *you*!"

She screamed so loud her voice cut out.

She flexed her fingers over the handle. Readied herself to do it.

This was it.

Nearly there.

"I do love you, Briony. I do. And I know I may not have shown it in–"

"You showed it."

"I did? Then why–"

"Because you only showed it when I fucked an older man."

"Oh, Briony, I didn't mean to–"

"You only showed it when I was hurt. But you showed it to Shane when he was angry."

"Oh, I didn't—"

"You showed it to Shane when *he* was angry, so why not me?" She tried to make her words make sense through her weeping, but she struggled to do so. "Why not me…"

She fell to her knees but kept the blade by her throat.

Mum stepped forward. Briony pressed the knife harder against her skin and a police officer put a hand on Mum's arm to hold her back.

"Will you love me now I'm dead?" Briony asked.

"What? Of course I—"

"Will you mourn for me, knowing what I've become?" Her face twisted with another onslaught of tears. "Will you want me now you can't have me?"

"Briony, I always want you. There is nothing I want more than just lying next to you—"

"You loved Shane. He was like this all the time, and you loved him."

"Shane needed me more."

"*No he did not!*" She wiped her eyes with her spare arm. "He did not he did not he did not *he did not he DID NOT!*"

Mum twitched her arms, wanting to step forward, wanting to embrace her child, and Briony was tempted—for a moment—to run into those arms and cry into her mother's shoulder.

But it wouldn't last. They would handcuff her and take her away as soon as she did. They wouldn't let her go home.

And even if she was allowed to go home, this attention would only be temporary.

They would lie in bed and watch movies. Cuddle. Talk. Endlessly talk. Until the fuel that powered her mother's love ran out, or until Shane became angrier than she was—whichever came first.

"I'm sorry, Mum," she said, a whisper only the two of them heard.

It began raining. The early signs of another storm. There had been one earlier that night, and now it was returning. The patter on the pavement growing louder. Circles appearing in puddles where water drops hit them. The smell of fine rain warning of more to come.

"Briony, please. Don't do this. Don't…"

She looked into her mother's eyes.

Deep into those eyes.

Blue, like hers.

And she dragged the knife across her throat, blood squirting into the rain. She fell to her knees and collapsed as a gaping wound the width of her neck stole her breath.

Her mother rushed to her side, desperate to help, but was ushered out of the way by the officers.

Paramedics pressed their hands on the wound, trying to stop the bleeding, trying to keep her breathing.

She was put into the back of an ambulance.

The police escorted the ambulance to the hospital with Beatrice on the backseat, sat in the place where many prisoners had sat. She watched the back of the ambulance for the entire journey, knowing that her daughter was tiptoeing across the fine line between dead and alive.

TEXT MESSAGES RETRIEVED FROM BRIONY SPECTOR'S PHONE

I love you Briony

Please survive this

Please

I'm waiting for them to tell me

They are operating on you

And I can't stand it

I promise I will tell you how much I love you

I promise I will tell you every day

I am sorry

Just please survive this

Please survive this

Please

CHAPTER THIRTY-NINE

She was wheeled in on a gurney, artificial lights rushing past, marble floor beneath squeaky wheels, past beige clinical walls and posters about washing hands and worn-out nurses rubbing their tired eyes.

Police trailed behind.

Doctors spoke—medical jargon—*We have an eighteen-year-old girl deep laceration across her throat yada yada yada*—running as fast as one could with four people's hands on a gurney—as fast as one can with the furious steps of nurses behind them—with eyes appearing in doorways to watch—faces leaving waiting rooms to see—strangers gossiping with strangers—visitors posting photos online.

Is that her?

The one from the news?

There's no way they can save her from that.

Why did she do it?

Didn't you hear?

She was a psycho.

Into A&E. Hooked up to a machine. She was unwillingly clinging onto life.

For the police, they needed someone alive to face justice.

For the mother, she needed someone alive to quell her guilt.

For the doctors, they just needed someone alive.

The senior doctor took the lead. Secured the airway. A tracheostomy tube at the distal tracheal end. Demanded that a nurse find her blood type. *Decreasing pulse.* There was a large hematoma. *Get me that blood dammit—get me that blood!* Began intravenous crystalloids. *Where is that fucking nurse?* Gave her anaesthetic. *I knew I should have called in sick today.* There was partial transection of the right internal jugular vein and—*fuck it's on the left side as well*—the whole vein—the whole jugular—the entire thing is—*there's no fucking way we'll save this girl*—he needed a tube for better ventilation—*yes get the blood in her now don't fucking wait around*—vitals were…

Nowhere near stabilised.

Her pulse was dropping.

The doctor changed their gloves. Too bloody already. They were slipping and sliding.

Bilateral sternocleidomastoid not intact.

Sutures for the oesophagus.

Need round sutures, not those ones, round ones.

Surgical knots outside the lumen.

It's already ripped, the gap is too wide.

Beep. Beep. Beep. Nowhere near steady. Beep. Beep. Too far apart. Beep. Getting further and further apart. Beep.

Fuck it!

She flatlined.

Fucking shit!

Outside the room, beyond the guarding officers, a mother couldn't sit down. She held her face in her hands. Pacing. One side of the corridor to another. Walked into someone trying to get past with a coffee. Didn't apologise. Glanced at the police.

They looked away.

She was the enemy.

Guilty by association.

Why hadn't she done her job? Why hadn't she brought her up better? Why had one of their colleagues died because of her?

No. She shook her head. No, no, no. Briony was a good girl. He must have done something to her first. He must have deserved it. She can't have done the things they said, can't have, she can't have, she–

Why was that beep still going? Was that a flatline? Is she flatlining?

Oh, Briony…

She ran toward the room. Police stepped in front of her. Two burly men blocking her way. She wanted to see her daughter. They said no. She was dying. Their faces were grim. Uninterested. Of course they were.

Her daughter was a murderer.

No. Must have a reason. She was a good girl. A good girl.

Meanwhile, a widow sat on the edge of a bed in a room two floors up and a building across. Her wrist was fractured from being hogtied for over three hours. She was being treated for minor injuries. She'd just been told that Kevin didn't make it. But she already knew. So she didn't cry out, didn't make a scene, didn't weep hysterically—she just bowed her head, closed her eyes, and prayed for answers.

Shortly after, the doctors told Beatrice the news.

It had been a long shot. The cut was deep. It was half her throat. There had only been a faint heartbeat to begin with, it didn't matter how soon they'd brought her in. And it didn't matter how kindly they told her. She still broke down. Still threw her fists at anyone who stood in her way. Still blamed them for everything.

A few hours later, the morgue welcomed a pretty girl who made a hideous corpse.

She lay on another gurney. A metal one. A cold one, but no colder than her. Her future was left flat and stiff and soon to be cremated.

She was dead. We're done. The end.

What more is there to say about Briony Spector?

There are many things, but most would be speculation. She was an ordinary girl in an ordinary family with ordinary problems. She didn't fit in. She did fit in. She worked hard. Sometimes she didn't. She was your daughter, your sister, your predator, your prey.

She could have been anything she wanted.

She could have been the doctor who tried to save her life. She could have been the police officer who pulled her away. She could have been the teacher who didn't know what to do.

She could have loved, and loved hard. She could have been a wife. Had children. She could have been gay, straight, happy, sad, loved, wanted—she had the potential to be anything and everything.

But that was *potential.*

There is no certainty there.

Suggestions, yes, but no certainty.

Indeed, there are a great many things you could say about what Briony Spector might have been, there is only one thing you could say for certain about her; something you could state without so much as an inclination of doubt—that she was completely, unequivocally, unmistakably remarkable.

And she will remain remarkable forever.

JOIN RICK WOOD'S READER'S GROUP...

And get three eBooks for free

Join at **www.rickwoodwriter.com/sign-up**

HAVE YOU READ ALL THE BLOOD SPLATTER BOOKS?

BLOOD
SPLATTER
BOOKS

HE EATS
CHILDREN

RICK WOOD

18+

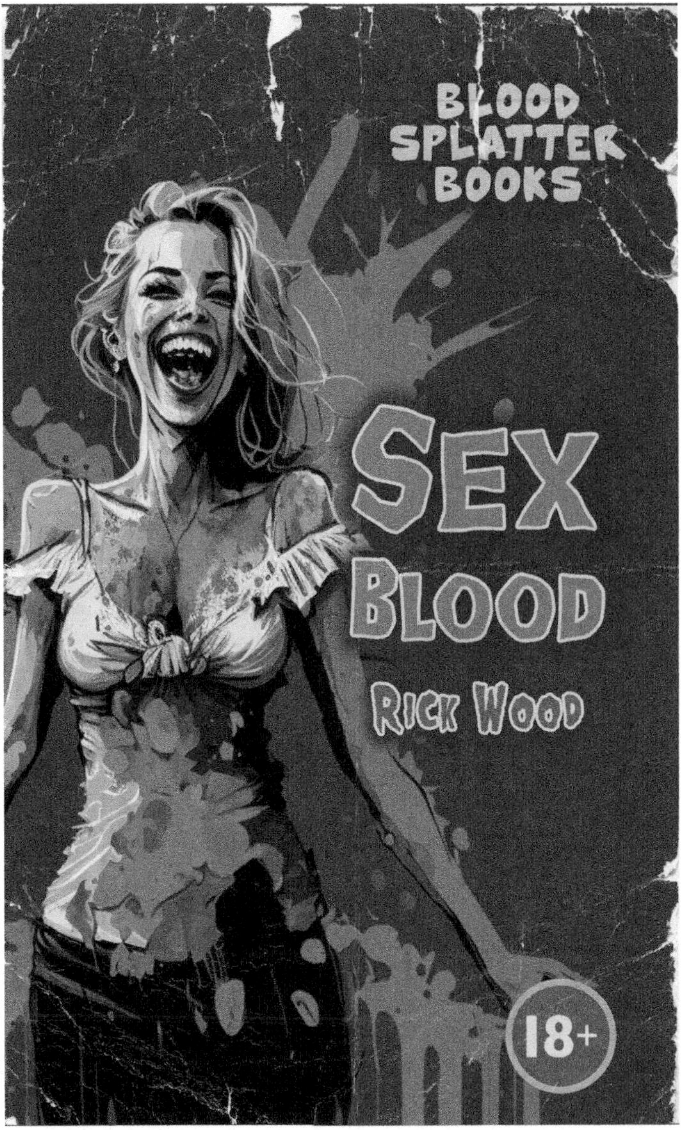
BLOOD SPLATTER BOOKS
SEX BLOOD
RICK WOOD
18+

BLOOD SPLATTER BOOKS

This Book is Full of Bodies

Rick Wood

18+

BLOOD
SPLATTER
BOOKS

WOMAN
SCORNED

Rick Wood

18+

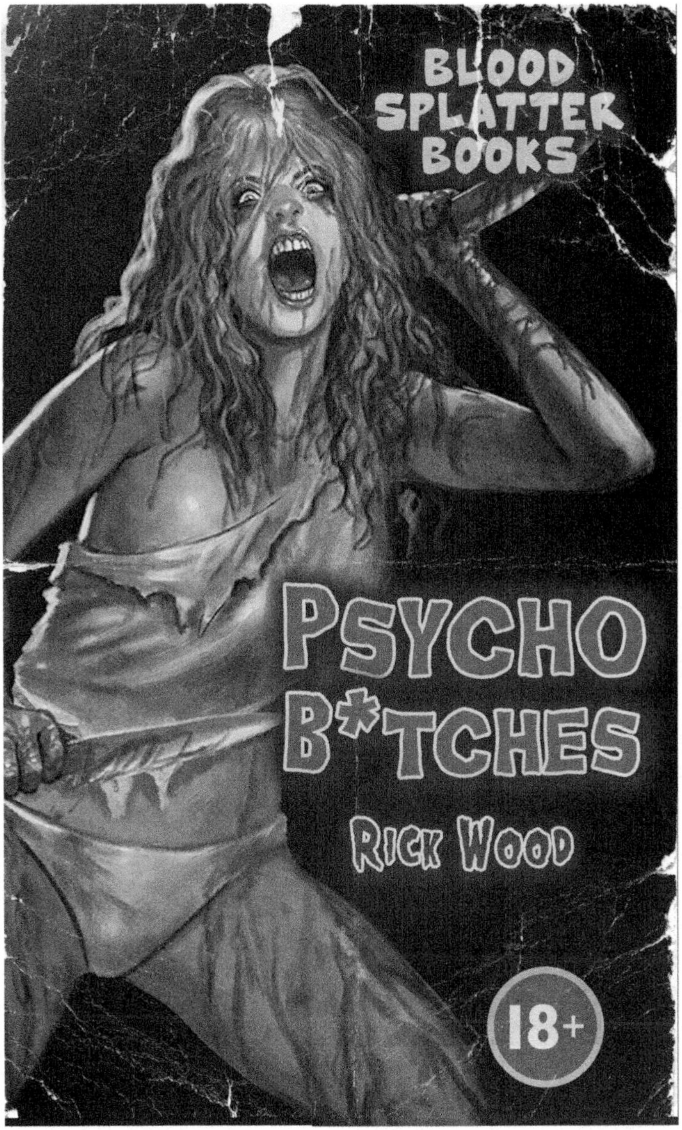
BLOOD SPLATTER BOOKS
PSYCHO B*TCHES
RICK WOOD
18+

BLOOD SPLATTER BOOKS
HAUNTED HOUSE
Rick Wood
18+

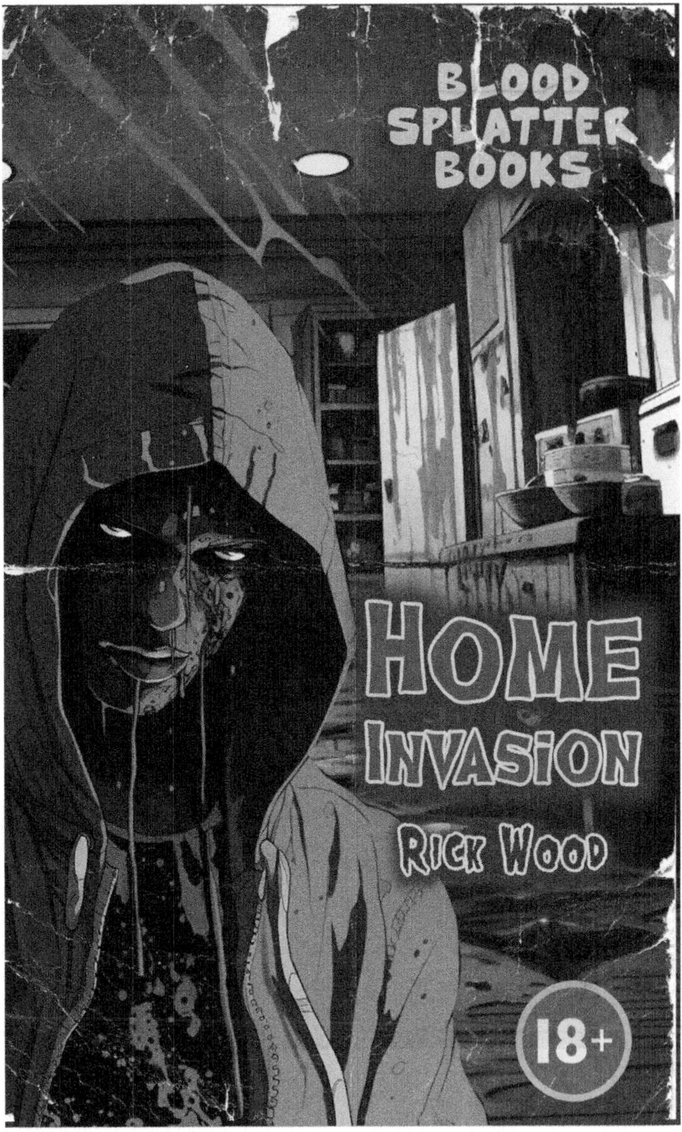
BLOOD
SPLATTER
BOOKS
HOME
INVASION
RICK WOOD
18+

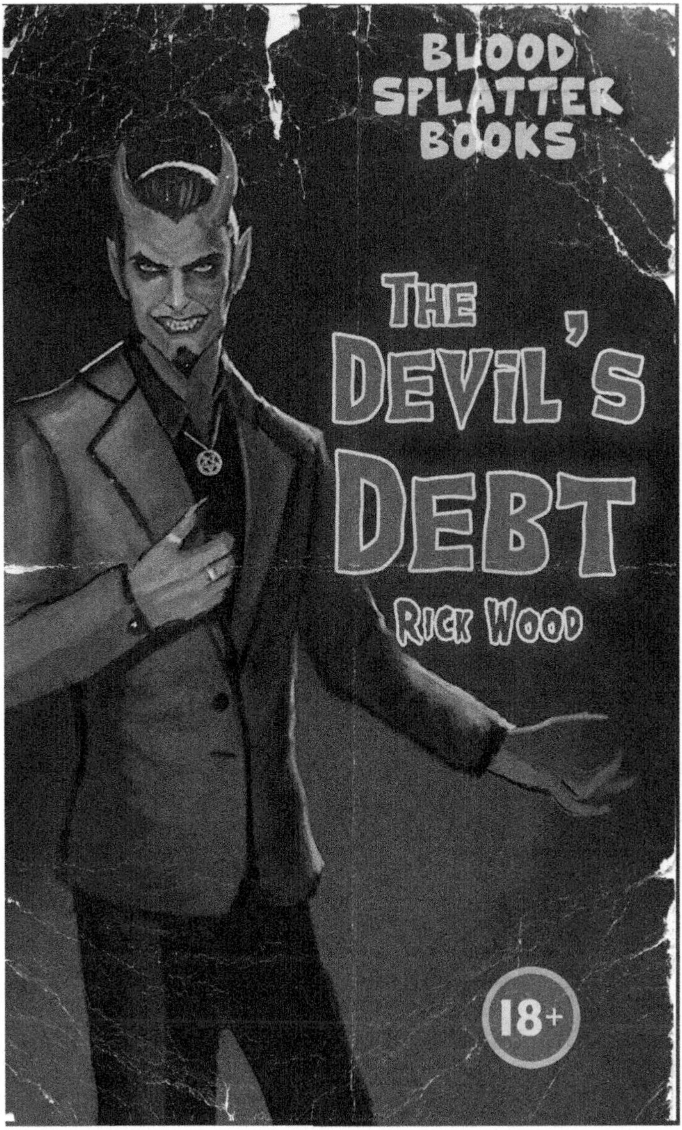
BLOOD SPLATTER BOOKS
THE DEVIL'S DEBT
RICK WOOD
18+

BLOOD
SPLATTER
BOOKS

SHUTTER
HOUSE

RICK WOOD

18+

Printed in Great Britain
by Amazon